Confessions
Kinky Divorcee

LANA FOX

mischief

This novel is entirely a work of fiction.
The names, characters and incidents portrayed in it are
the work of the author's imagination. Any resemblance to
actual persons, living or dead, events or localities is
entirely coincidental.

Mischief
An imprint of HarperCollins*Publishers*
77–85 Fulham Palace Road,
Hammersmith, London W6 8JB

www.mischiefbooks.com

A Paperback Original 2013

First published in Great Britain in ebook format by
HarperCollins*Publishers* 2012

A catalogue record for this book is
available from the British Library

ISBN-13: 9780007553372

Set in Sabon by FMG using Atomik ePublisher from Easypress

Find out more about HarperCollins and the environment at
www.harpercollins.co.uk/green

Contents

CHAPTER ONE

Pussyfooting

Thursday, 1 March

Dear Kitten,

I know your new name sounds silly, Kitten, especially considering you're only a notebook, but how can I begin every sex-crazed confession with the words 'Dear Diary'? Even Anais Nin didn't do that. Anyway, once you've heard what I've been up to recently, you'll probably be pushing me to quit the shoe biz and commit to my calling as a writer of smut. But let's start with the basics. Why 'Kitten'? you ask. Well, as soon as I saw your tiger-fur cover, I was smitten, Kitten. You reminded me of those tiger-print stilettos I've been saving up for – even with my staff discount it'll be weeks before I can buy them. But if anything would make me feel like a goddess, it's those.

Anyway, 'Tiger' seemed like a bad name for a

sex-confession diary – after all, I don't want to share my secrets with some savage animal. So yes, you will be my kittenly confidante, because I may not be able to share my kinky secrets with anyone else. But you – with your furry cover? I'm up to the task.

So. Secret number one.

Just one year ago, when I first found those pale-blue lacy knickers in Henry's suit pocket, my heart didn't break even slightly. That's the real tragedy.

See, it felt like I *should* have been broken by this, him being my husband, but nope, his having a 'bit on the side' didn't even surprise me. Instead, I stretched those flimsy things out and gazed at them, imagining the curvy body of the woman they belonged to. Skimpy little things that cup the bum cheeks. And between you and me, Kitten, I just had to bury my face in them – to find out how a woman smells. And this one smelled so musky, so deliciously off-bounds, that I felt myself getting damp. *Wet.* That's right. Burning between the thighs too, like the times when Henry actually bothered to screw me. In fact, I was so turned on that I wanted to meet this lay of Henry's, this bit on the side, and touch her and taste her, push my tongue inside her, like a tabby with a tub of cream. I wanted to make her simper and tremble and beg me to, well … fuck her! Is that obscene? Gotta get used to saying the word. Fuck, fuck, fuck. Why the heck not? I don't think I care anymore.

Anyhoo, after that came some crying, and a few friends who said, 'Debs, he's eight years younger than you, what did you expect?'

I expect faithfulness, for starters, I'd say! It isn't like he'd asked me for an open relationship where I could get bouncy with muscular boys for a hundred pounds a pop.

Truth was; the end had come.

So why not go out with a bang?

Well, it was easy enough to park outside his workplace on Friday night and follow him as he pulled away from his so-called 'Friday drinks with the crew'. I tracked him in my Mini. A right little secret agent, I was. And when we arrived at a tiny cottage, with ivy trailing down the walls and porcelain dogs in the window, he parked the car, strode up to the front door and – get this, Kitten! – let himself in with a key.

I was out of that car lickety-split, nose against the front window. But they weren't in the front room and, when I looked through the letterbox, they weren't in the hallway either. Only when I scooted round the back of the house and crouched in front of one of the back windows, my court heels sinking down into a flowerbed, did I see them together. Henry sat calmly on the white leather sofa, his arm along the back, while she stood in front of him dressed in a short beige mackintosh, with a bowler hat and a pair of black stilettos. Her legs and thighs were bare – and, dear God, so tanned and slender! – and beneath her hat she was a stunning bleach-blonde.

I have never seen anyone in all my days that made me burn like she did, and I longed to keep watching, so I sank to my knees, ducking down low to keep myself hidden. And there was Henry, appraising her slowly, his gaze all gleaming and wicked while he beckoned her to come closer. The bastard had never looked at *me* that way! He'd been lying to me, all that time, while I was longing for a sex life! All those silky nighties I'd bought! And all for nothing!

But once she was right in front of him, one foot raised and planted on the couch next to him, all I could do was gape at her slender legs, and the way the mac fell apart at the join, revealing her inner thigh. And when Henry leaned forward and slid a hand up and down her shin, watching the path of his fingers, while he murmured some quiet command, I wished I was in his place. Then, slowly, she undid the buttons on her mac, holding his gaze until it slid to the floor and her bare body stood before me, all supple skin, high breasts and oh-so-hard nipples.

Then, in an instant, Henry was unzipping his flies and pulling her hips towards him so she fell into his lap, her knees either side of his. I heard her little cry of pleasure – like a girl at Christmas – and for just a moment I saw his cock in his hand before she sank down onto it, so the tip disappeared into her neatly trimmed … you know

… (yes, all right, I can do this) … into the trimmed hair of her pussy.

There. See? Bring on the smut.

Anyway, soon she was riding him and his hands were on her hips, pulling her down over and over, his stare big and dark as it glossed that beautiful body, resting for a while on those lovely, leaping breasts. He'd never looked at *me* with such gargantuan lust! But it didn't bother me really – it was the woman I wanted to watch. Dear heaven, I'd never seen another woman's bosoms during sex and I could see what all the fuss was about. They were so voluptuously full, and their bouncing was so keen, so pretty, so utterly obscene, especially when accompanied by her sweet little cries – cries that grew breathier as she rode him. She had a wonderful bottom too. So shapely and firm. So mesmerised was I that I hardly noticed Henry's grunting – I was imagining I was Henry and that she was riding *me*, slicking it up with every thrust. I'd cup a breast, if it were me, pressing a nipple in my palm, while with my other hand I pawed a single buttock … or maybe even slapped it. And as I thought this, I found my fingers creeping beneath my skirt, so I burrowed deeper, shamelessly slipping inside my briefs. But it wasn't just my fingers that made me come. It was her glazing gaze, the way she threw back her head, her curls dancing down her back. And the thread of moisture that had crawled across her thigh and was creeping towards her stiletto shoes – because she was too wet to hold it in, while her hips pumped up and down, faster and faster still …

See? Pure *Penthouse*. Actually, Kitten, I wonder how well they pay …

But that was before I told him to leave. That was before the end. His end, not my end, mind. I wasn't the one that screwed it up. Then again, Kitten, since I'm meant to be confessing, I felt like I'd strayed too. Just watching that girl sliding up and down on him … wasn't that infidelity, in its way?

Anyway, Henry moved out and we were divorced within a couple of months – that's ten months ago now. I gave him everything he wanted, just to end our marriage *tout de suite*. And once he'd gone, things were fine for a while. Except that I grew lonely, just me with my shoe collection and not enough cash to restock it.

I was promoted to shop manager at Pussyfoot's Chipham branch, but my salary still wasn't enough to live on happily, so I had to sell the Mini. Broke my heart, it did. And you know; it's hard managing a shoe store when you lust after shoes but can't afford to buy them. That's why my friend Gladys persuaded me to get myself a tenant. Of course, Gladys, whose current project is to show me that turning forty will make me sexier than ever, thought I'd find myself a young student of the male variety – a boy half my age who goes to the local uni and studies motor mechanics or some other suitably macho profession.

Then along came Janey Prince in her ripped jeans and pageboy cap, sitting quietly at my kitchen table. And with her intense blue eyes and cropped blonde hair she was more of a stud than any man I'd known. I gave her the Jessica Rabbit mug and she raised her eyebrows at it, before bringing it to her lips and taking a sip.

'You'll need a sense of humour if you're going to live with me,' I said.

She watched me, owl-like, head tipped to the side. 'I'm more the quiet type,' she said, in a voice that could melt butter.

I asked her what she did, and she told me she was a gender studies student at the local university. 'Don't you want a *student* house?' I asked.

'I'm not really into people my age,' she said, simply.

'Why not?' I said. 'Kids should be kids.'

She gave me a glare. 'I'm twenty-three.'

I could hardly look at her, I was so embarrassed. 'It's a turn of phrase,' I told her, 'that's all.' But inside I was thinking, Like hell am I going to live with a humourless student who probably smokes too much grass and judges my every word! But there was something about her. She gave off this glow. That's the only way to put it. So I said, 'I was only thinking you'd probably pay less rent in a student house.'

She shrugged one shoulder. 'My parents are both dead. They left me money. I can do what I like with it. And like I say, I'm not usually into people my age.'

Oh, God, Kitten, the poor kid! She flushed and stared fixedly at Jessica Rabbit, turning the mug a little as if she wanted a better view.

'I'm sorry,' I said, gently. 'Blah, blah, blah, that's me. I shouldn't pry, should learn to engage my brain.'

She gives a small smile.

'Anyway,' I say, 'What do you do in gender studies?'

And then she cheered up a little. 'For my dissertation,' she said, looking up from beneath her lashes, 'I'm writing about the history of the stiletto heel.'

Holy smoke! I could have shot through the ceiling!

'Well, there you go! I work in a shoe shop.'

'Yeah?' Her eyes brightened. 'Which one?'

'Pussyfoot,' I told her.

And, dear God, she gave me a dazzling smile! Her eyes shone as if someone had lit a candle inside her. 'I love that shop!' she said, clapping her hands together. 'My girlfriend Lil shops there. She loves shoes – we both do.'

Girlfriend? So Janey was a lesbian, then. I'd never met a lesbian before. Suddenly, in my head, I was back with my knees in the soil, gazing in at the woman who was riding my naked husband. And just for a moment – you won't believe this, Kitten – I replaced Henry with Janey, so that she was the one with the big long cock, except it was one of those strap-ons, I suppose. And in this daydream, as the lithe woman bounced away, Janey turned and glared at me – but it was a sexy glare, an 'I want you' glare. Dear God. The thought of it made me flood.

Janey took a sip from the Jessica Rabbit mug, and I sat back, glancing down at her feet, and asked her to show me her shoes. She raised a leg, revealing a light-blue baseball boot. What a letdown! I raised an eyebrow. 'D'you wear those when you're studying the history of the stiletto?'

'When I'm studying the stiletto,' she said, 'it's my *girlfriend*'s shoes I watch.' Then she looked right at me, as if she was saying, *Picture it.*

And just like that, I was wet.

'Show me yours,' she said, at last.

It took me a moment to work out what she meant – and when I did, I couldn't resist standing up and giving a little walk to show my beauties off. Classy black peep-toe heels with supersoft leather – perfect for any kind of business transaction – and she stared at them, her eyes darkening, before letting her stare gloss my legs, my thighs, my blouse, then finally returning to the shoes. 'They're hot,' she said, in a husky voice that made my insides give a little. 'You wear them well.' And just like that, I was imagining her kissing my feet.

'The rent's four hundred a month,' I said.

She nodded, 'The room's perfect. Lil would stay over a couple of nights a week, but you'll hardly know she's there.'

'Any girl who loves shoes is a friend of mine,' I told Janey.

So that was that. Janey moved in yesterday.

Well, why am I writing this diary, you ask? Why confess my erotic thoughts about a twenty-something to a blank page? Because I'm worried about myself, Kitten. I mean, I still dream about men, don't get me wrong. But now I also dream about Janey in a strap-on, sitting on the bed, watching as I parade about in skimpy knickers and high-heeled shoes, that serious stare of hers soldered on mine. And, just like Henry, I've always been ... you know, sceptical ... about girls dating girls. I always wondered what they'd *do* together. Henry said that too. 'What does anyone do without a cock, my dear?'

But what if I want to find out? After all, I'm not his 'dear' any more. And you know what it said in my stars last week? 'Now look here, you roving Archers,' said Evita Grant, my astrology guru, when I flicked to her page in my copy of *Fashion Femme*. 'Don't you go using your secret shame as an excuse to flee. Whatever you've been repressing, now's the time to heal it. Come out, come out, come out! Commit to being you.'

Well, that's Evita. Sometimes, I wonder if, when she looks at the night sky, the stars spell out words that I just can't see.

10

Shameful secret number two: when I went to bed last night, I left my peep-toe shoes by the front door, like I often do. The last thing I expected was what I saw, next morning. There I was, about to walk down the stairs, when I noticed Janey Prince in the entrance hall below me, kneeling on the carpet, wearing nothing but a black T-shirt. She was totally in profile, so I could see the swell of her bum from beneath the black fabric, and her long, slender legs. In her hands she was holding one of my black peep-toe shoes, turning it, gazing at it, running a fingertip down the stiletto heel. I caught my breath, but she can't have heard, because she turned the shoe upside down and raised it to eye-level. She stared at the heel for a while before putting her face close and licking the length of it, slowly, giving a rough little growl.

Now, it's not like me to pussyfoot around watching others, but heavens, it was Janey who was invading *my* space, right? Oh, but I was mesmerised, Kitten, standing there in my dressing gown, my heart thumping away, wet between my thighs. What if she licked my heel like that while I was wearing the shoes? What if she lay on the floor, and I slid the heel between her lips and made her, you know, suck it? What if she writhed around, enjoying every inch? And what if this turned me on so much that the moisture slid down my thighs, while she stared at me, lustfully, as I slid that heel in and out?

So you know what I did, Kitten? After she put my shoe down and walked towards the kitchen, all pale thighs and bed-ruffled hair, I went to the bathroom and pushed my fingers inside me and thought about wearing that peep-toe shoe and pressing the heel inside her. I thought about fucking her with it, Kitten, over and over again, while she rolled around, naked, gasping with pleasure. She was so wet that the heel slid in easily and was coated with more moisture at every thrust. And I imagined her coming, Kitten, while she watched me fucking her like that. I imagined her long moan and the way she thrust her hips, slamming her arms against the floor as if to brace herself. I imagined her body arching so much that her firm little breasts rose towards me, and she moaned on and on.

But you know what shames me the most, Kitten? When I touched myself in the shower with my fingers deep inside me, I came like I've never come before. So hard and deep that I lost my balance, and had to grasp the shower curtain to stop myself from falling. And then I came again and again and again, in a crescendo, Kitten – just nothing but scorching pleasure, over and over, until, once I'd finished, I found I'd been writhing so much that I was caught in the shower curtain. It was wrapped and twisted around me like a badly clingfilmed haddock, because of just how hard I'd come.

I can't help wondering if Janey Prince heard me, Kitten,

even though she was downstairs. I was so loud, that she surely couldn't have missed it. And is it awful to say that the very idea made me touch myself again, and come again, hard, just to think of it?

That's why I got to work late, Kitten. Yes, I, the manager, arrived later than the staff! Pearl, my assistant manager, was watching me sideways all afternoon, a suspicious look in her soft brown eyes that seemed to say, 'I'm on to you.'

And I don't have to tell you which shoes I wore to work.

Not that I'm a lesbian, Kitten. At least ... no, I'm just playing with the thought.

But I haven't given Janey a contract, just in case I can't have her around, in case she spoils my career or puts me off men or makes a cradle-snatcher of me. Anyway, I suppose this is a trial period, really. Rent once a month. And I'll keep an eye on things. I mean, who knows if I'll be able to live with a twenty-three-year-old student?

And who knows if she'll be able to live with me?

CHAPTER TWO

A Well-Heeled Guy

Friday, 2 March

Dear Kitten,

Well, when I got home from work tonight, it was clear that Janey was properly moved in. The place smelled of incense, there was a dirty great footprint on the kitchen linoleum, and two new jackets – one in denim, one in leather – were hanging from the coat rack. But the real proof that my tenant was finding her feet was that I found her in the kitchen wearing tiny denim cut-offs that showcased her lovely thighs. She was chopping tomatoes with her earbuds in, and when I went over to say hello and tapped her on the shoulder, she almost hit the roof! That's me for you. Pure Sagittarius. Got about as much tact as a prize-winning marrow.

'Oh, I'm sorry, love,' I told her, putting my hand on her arm.

She shook her head, taking out an earbud. She smelled beautiful – of incense and coconut soap and fresh tomatoes. 'I'm glad of it,' she said. 'You interrupted the most boring podcast ever.'

'What's it about?'

'The stiletto heel.'

It turns out she was listening to some lunatic professor who thinks high heels are a sign of women's subjugation. 'Maybe some of us *want* to be subjugated,' I said, stealing a bit of tomato. When I looked back, she was shielding her grin with her fingers as if I'd said something delightfully naughty. Her eyes were what my friend Gladys would call fuck-you-blue. 'Things are only subjugation if you don't actually want them,' I said. 'I suppose I'd make a useless feminist.'

'Actually,' said Janey, 'that's the most feminist thing I've heard all day.' She smiled openly now, surprisingly sunny-faced. Her eyes really are a marvellous shade of blue.

'Well,' I said, 'I should rest my feet. These shoes of mine are killing me.' I noticed how her gaze immediately darted down to my shoes. 'See you later,' I said, turning away.

'Wait,' she said, catching my arm. 'Lil's coming by tonight. Is that OK?'

I said *of course* it was OK, she didn't have to ask. And I felt a little relieved, as I turned away, because seeing

Janey's girlfriend would break this silly crush of mine. But as I walked towards the hallway I could feel Janey's stare burning its way down the backs of my legs, and the sensation made me so lustful that I paused and glanced back. Her eyes were all big and gleaming, Kitten, as she drank in my burgundy five-inchers, teamed with sheer hose. She was so greedily fixated that it took her a moment to look back up at me. And when our gazes met, she didn't even flush. 'You have gorgeous shoes,' she told me, holding my stare, 'and beautiful legs. Did you know that?'

Oh, that gaze of hers was bold as brass. Inside my knickers, I burned. And as I mumbled a thank-you and turned away, I suddenly wondered if she'd stolen the shoes I was wearing and licked them while I wasn't around. Well, why wouldn't she? She's done it before. And the image of her staring at me with her tongue sliding over my heels made my pussy ache so much that I rushed to the bedroom and, with my back against the door, slipped my fingers into my knickers and rubbed myself hard. Just thinking of the burn in her stare made me come in moments. And just like every climax I have when I think about Janey, it was so hot and deep and hard that I cried out loud.

See, Kitten? I'm like the *Story of O*. (But without the whipping, obviously.) This girl is young enough to be my own daughter. Is this my future sex life? Me getting older, while my tastes get younger?

16

Anyway, I have to dress up now. I'm meeting Gladys for drinks this evening. She's been dating a swish American man called Guy, so there's bound to be gossip. I'll spill the beans when I get back.

10.50 p.m.

Oh, Kitten, what a night! I don't know whether to be excited or embarrassed! See, the 'thing' Gladys said she wanted to show me turned out to be – but wait. Let me start from the beginning.

I arrive at the Queen's Head expecting a girls' night out, but, when I spy Gladys over in the corner, she's sitting next to a man in a swanky suit. Oh, God, I think to myself. She's brought the guy she's been dating. Typical Gladys. Her boundaries are so stuffed up. Anyway, as I strut towards her, feeling hot-as-heck in my silver stiletto heels, I'm not so sure it *is* her man. Gladys is a flirt-and-a-half, and men always enjoy her, but she's sitting upright in her 'teacher' pose. She's wearing an Eastern-style dress, which works beautifully next to her dark skin. It's a stunning shade of red with gold-and-white dragonflies embroidered on it, but it doesn't meet Gladys's criteria for a 'fuck-me dress'. For starters, it's buttoned up to the throat, with zero cleavage, and for seconds, she's wearing jeans underneath – a big no-no for Gladys when it comes to seduction. Her black hair is in hippie-style bunches, and, of course, her fingernails are perfectly painted. At the age of forty-nine, she's more 'Indian goddess' than ever. Even with the fine lines that spread from the corners of her eyes, and the laughter-lines that deepen when she laughs, Gladys Patel is still a forty-something going on twenty-nine.

And the men she dates are young – often early thirties. Take this guy she's with, for instance, with his gleaming brown eyes and broad jaw. He's the one who sees me first and mentions me to Gladys, who rises and welcomes me with a squeeze. With one arm around my waist, she introduces me to her 'friend' Guy, who gives me a saucy sideways grin before taking my hand and kissing my cheek. He smells delicious – of aftershave and gin – and, as he turns away from me, he gives me a quick wink. And oh, my, Kitten! What a wink it is! It gets me all wet and squirmy.

'Now,' says Gladys, once Guy has smoothly produced a chair for me, 'I want to introduce you both because of your interest in shoes.'

I gawp at her. What on *earth* is she talking about?

And, typical Gladys-style, she announces: 'He likes shoes in the sack, Debs. A foot fetishist. Like you.'

Like *me*? 'Gladys, I'm not a fetishist!'

Gladys raises her eyebrow as she lifts a half-pint to her lips. 'You once said you'd rather screw shoes than men. If that isn't a fetish, I don't know what is.'

I immediately flush. I don't even remember saying such a thing! Typical fucking Gladys to spill my intimate blurts, then tell the world about them.

Guy laughs and places a hand on my arm. A firm, warm hand – and very nice it is too. 'Gladys knows I love shoes,' he tells me, 'and apparently you work in the shoe biz.' His American accent is leisurely and smooth, and his eyes – oh, his eyes! – they're boring into me, as if they're seeing my fantasies.

I tell him I manage Pussyfoot Shoes, in town.

'I'd love to hear more about that,' he says, his pupils growing bigger as they pull me in. 'In fact, I'd love to see your style.' He glances down towards my feet. 'Show me your foot, Debs.'

When he says this, Kitten, several things happen. My whole face burns – as does my pussy. (See how easy that word's become, Kitten? If I'm not careful, *Playboy* will ask me to tea.) Gladys gives a snort, slams down her beer glass, mutters 'excuse me' through a snigger and runs off towards the women's loos. Guy twists towards me in his chair, then bends downwards and cups his hands as if to take my shoe in them. And his stare is so penetrating that I slip off my shoe and hand it over.

Now brace yourself for the weird bit, Kitten.

Guy gives a tiny groan as he takes the shoe. I might as well have placed my breast in his hands, the way he drinks it in, all ravaging and fierce. 'Perfect,' he says, softly, turning it and running a finger down the stiletto heel. He slips a hand inside it and feels up the inside, and I'm surprised to feel tingle in-between my thighs, as if he's fondling my ... pussy. (Oh, God, Kitten, whatever porny language will I let slip next?) 'Oh, yes,' he says, softly, and in the heave of his voice, I can tell he's hard. Then he cups the back of the shoe in his palm and holds it up to observe the whole thing. 'Oh, fuck, yes,' he murmurs in a kind of private dream, and then he looks at me like a wolf, his pupils swallowing the browns of his eyes, and says, 'You have exquisite taste. If you wear these in the bedroom, your boyfriend is a lucky boy.'

Of course, I'm so on the edge of my seat because of this captivating man that I blurt, 'I'm single,' like some kind of trollop.

'Good,' he says. 'Let's go to dinner. Tomorrow.'

'Tomorrow?'

Suddenly, Gladys is back, giving me a private wink. 'Do you two lovebirds need some time alone?' she says, looking like she might explode with the giggles.

'Don't be daft,' I tell her. 'I haven't even ordered my drink yet.'

Staring at me, Guy says, 'I would offer to go to the bar, but I'm so horny right now it would be indecent.'

Of course, Gladys thought this was a riot! And that's how it was all evening. Guy making hot little comments as he glared into my eyes, and Gladys giggling away or nudging my elbow, telling me Guy and I should date. And all the way through, as we talked about this and that, I'm imagining him throwing me down on the table and fucking me, as glasses and silverware crash to the floor. Besides, I was so hot and wet that it wouldn't have taken much to make me come. One thrust, two thrusts, three thrusts, Kitten, and I'd be high as a kite, soaring on an orgasm, as he fucked and fucked with my foot in his hand.

See what you're doing to me, Kitten? *Penthouse*, here we come.

Anyway, at the end of the night he asks for my number, and before I'm even home he's texting to arrange dinner. I accept his offer with as much grace as I can after a few wobbly drinks, and I'm still thinking about it later when I'm climbing the stairs to bed, my mug of cocoa in hand. But on my way to my room I'm brought to a standstill by the sound of soft moaning. Whatever next, Kitten? It looks like the gods heard my mission to explore all things sexy, and are bombarding me with hotness wherever I walk. As I stand there, I have to steady myself against the wall because the bathroom door is ajar and I can see Janey against the bathroom wall, kissing a woman – Lil, I presume. I've ended up just at the right angle to watch, and believe me, Kitten, watch I do. Their kiss is a rough one, and Janey's cheeks are flushed and her blonde hair is tousled, and her jeans are undone, and on top she's wearing a simple black bra. And though I can't see Lil, I can see her mouth, her jaw, and her jet-black hair as she kisses Janey, scratching her nails down the girl's lovely arms. Janey arches and looks agonised as Lil pulls down her jeans and reaches around to unclip her bra. And suddenly, Janey's breasts are spilling loose. Such perfect round little breasts, so smooth and pale, their nipples a dusty pink, that I find my fingers inching towards my thirsty pussy. I should leave, Kitten, go to my bedroom, shut the door, go to sleep. But now Lil is down on her knees and Janey's jeans are falling round her ankles, and I watch her as she arches and claws at the wall, her lashes flickering.

Well, after that, what's a woman meant to do? Once I've sidled quietly into my room, I don't really want my cocoa anymore, so I go to bed and climax harder than ever. In fact, all through the night, I have wet dreams about Guy screwing me on the restaurant table, with my legs in the air, while Janey, in nothing but her black T-shirt, licks my stiletto heel, murmuring, 'Oh, we shouldn't, we shouldn't,' over and over again.

CHAPTER THREE

Tongue-Tied Thai

Saturday, 3 March
6.30 p.m.

Oh, Kitten! Two sexy things happened today. The first was small and hot. The second was so hot that I had to get myself off at the store. But let's start at the beginning ...

First, I had the strangest dream. Oh, this was a doozy! In it, an angel with her hair in sexy plaits is wearing a French maid's outfit. (Dear God, even my subconscious is going all *Playboy*.) Her wings stick out of the back of her costume, somehow, and her halo is perfectly straight – in spite of the kinky gear. The angel has this gorgeous smile, all peaceful and kind. She takes my hands and tells me, 'Let go of your shame, Deborah, dear. That's the number one rule.'

And what I realise, when I wake up, is that I think I believe her.

This is what I realise when I wake up to noises in Janey's room – Janey sounds like she's digging for gold and finding bigger and bigger chunks the deeper she shovels. 'Oh, God,' she's crying, 'Oh, God, God, God … ' The bed frame – which I really ought to replace – is bashing against the wall, softly at first, and then louder and louder, like some scene from a steamy movie. And then, suddenly, something's changed – something very, very hot – and the bangs become louder and faster and harder, and Janey shouts, 'Oh, *fuck*, baby.' And once again, I'm burying my fingers inside me.

I climax like the clappers, Kitten. Oh. My. Gosh.

After this, I shower, dress and go to breakfast, thinking about Guy and the date we have this evening. Someone – hopefully Janey, not Lil – is making breakfast and the aroma of coffee is wonderful. It reminds me of Henry and the way he used to look after me, bringing me breakfast in the mornings, and croissants on Saturdays.

Still, he's gone. Get over it, Debs.

In the kitchen, my tenant's laptop is open on the table, next to an empty plate. On the screen is a picture of a giant red stiletto shoe. The headline of the article is WHY WE CAN'T LET GO OF OUR HEELS. Janey herself is standing at the coffee maker in a new, shorter T-shirt, which shows a tantalising glimpse of her wonderful buttocks in a pair of pale-blue Lycra briefs. And oh, my gosh, I so want to stroke those buttocks – tiptoe up and lean against her back, cupping each cheek and feeling her respond. If I did so, God knows what would happen. Perhaps she'd give a little jolt of surprise before leaning back into me, purring as she presses my hand against the outline of her breast. If I had a cock, Kitten, I'd sweep aside her briefs just enough to push myself into her and feel her, wet from Lil, her lovely muscles gripping this new bit of me as I slide in and out, harder each time. (Honestly! This 'diary' business is hard. I'm embarrassed just writing about my fantasies, and you're not even human.) And anyway, what does this penis envy say about me? Does it make me lesbian? Henry would call me a gender-bender – and he'd probably be right. But is that such a bad thing? Gender-bending, I mean? This is what I'm thinking in the kitchen, when Janey turns back towards her computer and jumps with surprise to see me there. 'Oh, gosh,' she says, laughing and rolling her eyes. 'You startled me. Again.'

I tell her I'm sorry. I'm so used to living alone. At least, for the past year anyway. 'Hard at work, I see?' I say, pointing at her laptop screen.

'Did you know "stiletto" means "needle" in Italian?' says Janey.

'Really?' This floors me a little. The things I don't know about shoes.

Janey walks to her laptop, coffee mug in hand. 'In the 60s, the fashion gurus tried to get rid of stilettos. But women weren't having it. Demand was so high that the shoe shops had to give in.'

'I wouldn't give up my high heels for anything,' I tell her.

'I wouldn't either,' says Jancy. 'If I wore them, I mean.' Then she looks me right in the eyes. 'What size are you?' she asks. 'Feet,' she adds, when I look at her blankly.

I tell her I'm a six. 'Why d'you ask?'

Turns out she bought Lil some sexy shoes, but the girl doesn't like them. Lil takes a size five, I take a size six. The sad thing is, she'd have given them to me, if we shared a shoe-size.

I all but gush my thanks, and Janey gives a small smile. 'I just like it that you appreciate these things,' she says, sitting back at her computer screen. And I felt a little disappointed that she didn't look down at my red, furry boudoir-slippers – with kitten heels, no less.

'I bet we've got some lovely shoes for Lil at Pussyfoot's,' I say, ever the saleswoman. 'You should drop by.'

'Oh, I will,' says Janey, looking up, gaze intense. 'Soon, in fact. And if Lil can't make it, you can model them for me.' She stares at me for a moment, her pupils blackening with meaning, before turning back to her screen.

And, once again, I'm wet because of my twenty-three-year-old tenant. I have *got* to get over this. If anyone found out, what would I say? I wish you had a padlock, Kitten, but you haven't, so that's that. You know, I think it's time I started packing you in my handbag, carrying you with me, scrawling my secrets on the sly.

Anyhoo, the other things that happened today were both shoe-related. I'd been at Pussyfoot Shoes for about an hour when I went to take a loo break. On my return, I find my Saturday girl, Cheryl Brown, prancing around the sale section in a pair of Jimmy Choos. Dressed in her Pussyfoot uniform, which, by the way, is the same as mine – a white blouse with a pink, flared skirt – she looks like a gangly flamingo as she tries to strut in six-inch heels that are far too small. What's more, some boy in saggy teenage clothes (I assume this is her boyfriend) is half-snorting, half-laughing behind his hand as she performs this whole pantomime. It wouldn't have been so bad if there hadn't been a woman waiting, shoe in hand, clearly after some help. And by the look of her reddened cheeks and pursed lips, she'd been waiting quite a while.

This is not the first time this sort of thing has happened with Cheryl. She's a sweet girl, but lazy, and she seems to think it's fine to leave customers waiting while she has her fun. I should have fired her, Kitten – after all, she's already had two warnings – but when I got her into the back room and her boy wasn't there to impress, she looked paper-pale, and I felt sorry for her. 'I love working for you, Deborah,' she said, her bottom lip all quivery. 'This is the best job I've had.'

So I gave her a formal warning and sent her back to the shop floor. What a softie I am, Kitten. I wish I could be all strict and pro, like they are at Shoes by J down the street. People come from all over the country to shop at Shoes by J. The managers have more self-control than I have – and there's no way they wouldn't fire Cheryl on the spot. Maybe this weakness of mine is why I lost Henry, Kitten. I didn't assert myself. I just let him treat me like I didn't exist.

What's more, those poor Jimmy Choos that Cheryl had toyed with were so stretched that I had to take ten pounds off the price. My gosh, I love those shoes. They're black and lilac with steel heels. Steel heels! Delicious. Someone put care into those, Kitten. Mark my words, they were made with love.

Thank heaven for this afternoon, when an elegant man walks into the store. He's like a jaguar in his stylishness – all designer suit and cool stance. It's raining outside, which is why I wasn't expecting many customers. Besides, Cheryl's popped out for a coffee break and Pearl, my other member of staff, must be in the stockroom. So I dash over to help him, but when I get close he gives me a dazzling smile and I realise it's Guy. He kisses me on the cheek, takes my hand and says, 'Just thought I'd stop by and make sure we're good for tonight,' and he holds my gaze with those deep-brown peepers that swallow you up before you've even breathed.

I tell him I haven't forgotten. He's picking me up around seven.

'Ready for a little spice?' he says, raising a single eyebrow. It takes me a moment to get it – we're eating Thai tonight.

'I'm all about spice,' I say, gesturing towards the central display, where shoes rest on fur-trimmed shelves, their gold inner soles gleaming in the light.

I feel a glow of pride as Guy wanders across to the shoes. And guess which ones he reaches for first? The tiger-print stilettos! Kitten, I almost die. 'I've been saving up for those,' I say. 'They're rather too … dear for me.'

'Well, my *dear*,' he says, with a wink that makes me smile, 'let's see how you look in them.' And before I've had a moment to object, he's down on one knee, sliding my stockinged foot out of my pink three-inchers and into the tiger-print beauties. His fingers on my ankle make my legs tingle and the tingle shoots up my thighs, making me giddy and light. He gives a long 'Mmm' while he strokes the arch of my foot, as he places me into the shoe. And I must say, he handles me beautifully! So firm and in control, with just the right touch. When the delectable shoes are on, he even runs a hand down one of my calves, giving a breathy sigh. As he rises again, his gaze burns on my feet and legs, and oh, my gosh, I'm more turned on than ever!

He tells me to model them, and off I strut, proudly

showing off these high-heeled beauties. There's something of Janey Prince in his stare, and when I return to him my cheeks are burning at being watched like this. With a sideways grin, he sinks to one knee again and says, 'Give me your left foot, beautiful.' I have to check for customers before placing a fully clad foot onto the bridge of his knee and thigh.

He gives the tiniest groan as I grind my heel into his flesh, and when he runs a finger across the furry material, then down the needle-thin six-inch heel, I notice that I'm not the only one who's horny: the bulge in his grey suit trousers is big – oh, very big, Kitten! The kind of 'big' that sends a girl to the moon!

Then suddenly, he's getting up again and asking for the bathroom. I admit, I feel rather abandoned when I show him round the back to the staff toilet. But I know he still has his stiffy, so something tells me to listen at the door. Well! I only have to wait half a minute before I start hearing his moans, rising one after the other, interspersed by a sort of chafing, which I guess is his hand working that sizeable cock of his. 'Yeah,' he groans, in that sexy American drawl, 'Oh, fuck, yeah, press the heel right into it.' And I get wetter and wetter as I listen to him coming, shouting: 'All over your feet, all over your fucking feet …' before crying out, long and low, like some kind of wounded animal.

I scamper off as soon as the noise dies down, and to

my shame there is an unserved customer waiting at the counter on my return. I flush but greet her smilingly, reach down to the shelf below the counter and hand over the box of gold princess sandals that were waiting to be picked up. And as I ring her sale up, I see Mr Coming-All-Over-Your-Feet swaggering towards the shop door, calling, 'See ya at seven, angel,' as he gives a wave.

So, I've been soaking wet all afternoon, and now I'm about to get ready for Guy to pick me up. Have I touched myself? No! And it's your fault, Kitten! What would I rather do? Touch myself or write to you? Is it awfully bizarre to say the latter? It's as if giving you all my darkest secrets releases me somehow, makes me game to be myself. Anyway, I've decided to start carrying you with me in my bag. That way, I can update you whenever I like, and no one gets to see my *Playboy* bunny fantasies.

8 p.m.

Holy mackerel, Kitten, I'm just popping to the ladies to give you the latest! We're at the Thai Garden, and he's plied me with some kind of fancy white wine. Well, I let him ply me, let's face it. I'm a pushover for Chardonnay, so I admit I'm a bit tipsy. Maybe that's why Guy seems so sizzlingly irresistible.

But I have to hurry, so here's a quick list, before I forget the story …

1. He picks me up in the most exquisite Mercedes – a silver convertible with seats that smell of leather – and, rather than just tooting his horn like Henry would have, he parks the car, comes to the door and greets me in person. 'You look positively stunning,' he says, when I answer the door. And adds, 'A perfect wet dream.' How lovely it is to be craved by this smartly suited thirty-something with eyes that undress me … starting – or maybe ending – with my gold, evening sandals. Seriously, these have stiletto heels to die for.

2. As he drives, he lounges there like a jaguar, a single hand leisurely draped on the wheel. I tell him what Janey said about women in the 60s who wouldn't allow stilettos to disappear from the stores. He laughs, then says, 'Women who wear heels are hard to say no to.' Then he glances down at my flirty dress teamed with nylons, saying, 'Especially when they're as delectable as you.'

3. OK, Kitten, I've got to run now or he'll think I have the kind of problems only fibre can fix. The waiters and waitresses, who aren't all Thai by any stretch, are dressed in white with blue flowers in their hair. Also, there are coloured paper lanterns in red, gold and blue, and there's a huge tank filled with tropical fish. Guy's ordered us prawn crackers, spring rolls,

little shrimp toasts with chili sauce. All gorgeous! And I do love Chardonnay, especially when it's cold and served in crystal glasses, while the stud across the table presses his leg against mine.

4. I have to go now, Kitten. Back in a few ...

10.50 p.m.

Well, that was quite a date. He was utterly charming, dreadfully seductive, and his clear interest in bedding me made quite a delicious distraction. That man has eyes that bore through your clothes and touch your flesh – not softly, but firmly, as if you're an avocado and he's checking to see if you're ripe. But the most exciting thing was talking to him about shoes! Henry never took an interest in my shoe collection, or much else of mine for that matter. Guy, on the other hand, asked for the details of my every pair, not to mention my job at Pussyfoot Shoes and the women I serve. Now I'm not a fool, Kitten! I know he wants to imagine me touching women's feet, and getting aroused by it or something. But the thing about Guy is how direct he is. Here's an example ...

I get back from the ladies to find our main courses in front of us – prawns with basil and chili for me; beef in tamarind sauce for him. As we start to eat, I feel him watching me, but I don't rise to it straightaway – partly because I like him admiring me, and also because OH, MY GOD, THAI FOOD IS GORGEOUS! (Why has no one ever mentioned this before? All spices and sweetness and heat.) Anyway, finally he puts down his chopsticks, takes a swig of wine and leans towards me properly. 'I hope you don't think me rude,' he says, 'treating you so directly. I find you very attractive. And the fact that you have such taste in shoes … well, frankly, I got hard the moment I met you and haven't calmed down since.'

I flush, unable to meet his gaze. 'Oh my,' I say, 'you're very forward, aren't you.'

'It's my way of saying, "This is who I am."' He pauses for a beat, as I look into his eyes. Then, with the most devilish smile I've ever seen, he murmurs, 'I want to screw you, Deborah. Over and over again. And as I think you know, we'll be leaving your shoes on.' If I don't feel the same, he says, I should speak up now. Like Gladys would, God love her.

I laugh. 'That's Gladys for you.'

'I'm not really thinking of Gladys right now,' he says, pressing his knee against mine. Oh, gosh, his attention is wonderful! It makes me feel all precious and twinkly – I haven't felt like that in years. But I don't know how to respond. And I know I should hint that I'm not a sex-on-the-first-date girl. Suddenly, I don't want to look at him, so I gaze at the fish tank by the entrance, where large fish in all sorts of colours spread their glamorous fins.

'I'm embarrassing you, aren't I?' he says, at last. 'Forgive me. It's the Dom in me. I should share some more about myself. Let me tell you about my own workplace.'

He talks on and on about his big fancy office, but I'm not really listening. I'm full of delicious spices and the feel of his breath when he leans in close, and the way he talks about his clients as if they don't matter a jot. What a lean, mean man! And oh, my gosh, how sexy! As for me, I notice how fascinated he seems by my own work situation. He wants to know story after story of shoe sales – including what sort of women buy what, and why.

Anyway, we eat dinner, exchange small talk and have coconut ice cream for dessert. Oh, my goodness! And when I insist on splitting the bill, we have a small tiff before he caves. 'Gone are the days when a man could buy a lady a meal,' he says, with a glare.

To which I say, 'Instead, we have the days when a woman can pay for whatever she darn well chooses.'

He raises one eyebrow, but a smile plays over his lips. 'You've caught my weakness, Deborah dear.'

'Control,' I say. And I have a sudden image of me sitting astride him riding up and down, while he grasps one of my shoes in his left hand and one of my breasts with his right. I'm going at it hard, with my wrists bound behind me, and he's glaring at me, fiercely, like an angry dog and his lips are parted and wet with saliva. And I ride and ride, letting out cry after cry as he groans beneath.

'All over your shoes,' he moans. 'All over your fucking shoes.' But he comes inside me, long and hard, calling out my name.

Anyway, Kitten, I digress. Let's fast forward to outside the restaurant, where I tell him he shouldn't drive because he's been drinking. 'I'm going to drive regardless,' he tells me, cool as butter, but he also reaches up and smoothes a curl of hair from my face. It's begun to rain a little, but it's more like a fine mist – like when film stars spray perfume into the air then walk through it, to make sure of an even coverage. (That's what it says in *Cosmo*. I'm more of a 'squirt and go' kinda gal. These Hollywood women have more time than sense.)

So I tell Guy, 'Fine, but I'm getting a cab.' I hold up my hand as he tries to interrupt me. 'I'm paying for it. No question.'

'I wasn't going to offer to pay. I was going to offer to stay.'

'You're a poet and you don't know it,' I say. (Terrible rhyme. Shoot me now).

'You're insufferable,' he tells me, but he's smiling a little, and his gaze softens thoughtfully as he cups the side of my jaw. 'I've been trying to find a woman like you for a very long time.'

Bingo, Kitten. I beam away. 'In that case,' I add, 'you won't mind if I take a rain-check on the staying over?' I explain that I haven't been with a man since my husband dumped me, and Guy's immediate response is to pull me into a hug. Totally unexpected from Mr Suave! 'Of course I understand,' he says, gently. 'I'm sorry if my sex-patter makes me seem like a bastard. I can be very patient, I promise.' And just as I get a lump in my throat, because I can't remember how long it's been since a man was actually sweet to me, I find he's taking my face in his hands and kissing me on the mouth – it's a soft-firm smoulder of a kiss that tastes of Thai ice cream. It's been years since someone kissed me with such hunger and affection. And phew, I tell ya, I could get used to this, Kitten! I enjoy it so much that when he pulls back I must look like an idiot with my gob hanging open and my eyes all bugged. He smiles before lifting my hand and kissing it. 'Promise you'll take that taxi,' he says. And, before I know it, he's walking away.

I get a cab home, and when I arrive there's a woman sitting on my doorstep in nothing but a loosely buttoned shirt that only just covers the tops of her thighs. She's petite and tanned, with a black Cleopatra bob, and she's smoking a cigarette with her slender legs crossed. At her side is a saucer – from my rambling rose set! – filled with cigarette butts. She's clearly been out here a while. She's a stunning girl and I'm transfixed for a while before realising the front door is ajar. I'll bet the hallway is filling with smoke – it'll take me a year to get that out of the curtains.

'Hi,' she says, on an exhale. 'You must be Deborah.'

'And you're Lil,' I say.

'Jackpot,' she says, turning her gaze away. And you know, I don't like her, Kitten. She's sullen, this one. To a girl with that kind of attitude, eye-rolls come as easy as pie.

'We don't smoke in this house,' I say.

She sighs, slowly raising her gaze. 'That's why I'm outside.'

I ask where Janey is and she says, 'How should I know?' before drawing on her cigarette again and saying, 'Look, I'm sorry. I don't mean to be rude. We've fought is all.' She watches me as she rises to her feet and shakes my hand. Her fingers are slender and cold. 'Janey's watching a movie.*Her* kind of movie.'

'Right,' I say. 'Well, I'm sure you'll sort it out.'

'Oh,' she says, 'I'm sure *I* will.'

On the way in, I make a point of closing the door. And you know what, Kitten? I don't bother to do it quietly.

In the living-room, Janey is asleep along the brown leather sofa, in the most lovely nightwear I've ever seen. Her tiny shorts are made of grey silk with polka dots all over them, and her matching top has spaghetti straps – one of which has slipped down her arm – and a trim of black lace. On the TV, a film plays along. There are gunshots and witty quips, but I take no notice. All I can see is this beautiful girl curled up on her side, an arm draped over the edge of the couch, loosely holding the remote control. Her skin is white as a pearl and, with her legs bent up towards her belly, her tiny shorts can't quite contain her buttocks. Honestly, they're so smooth and tight and curved that all I can think of is running my hands up her thigh and exploring that beautiful behind. And there's something so miraculous about the past few days – what with Guy asking me out, and Janey moving in – that I go a little zany. Down I sit on the sofa next to her, and, leaning over the bottom half of her body, I gently stroke a loose strap back into place. She doesn't even stir, though her breath changes a little and she makes a tiny moan.

Oh, dear God! Burning to touch more of her, I whisper, 'Janey?' and when I get no response I rest a hand on her waist. When this doesn't wake her, I slide my palm round the dip of her hip, down to her perfect buttock, and I gently stroke her there, exploring the tight flesh. Oh, Kitten! I'm an abuser! I'm guilty of assault! But my pussy is burning so powerfully as I stroke and explore that I can't seem to stop, and Janey lets out more little moans of pleasure – obviously she thinks I'm Lil. And she even whispers, 'Oh, God, spank me,' as she rolls onto her front – and even though it's nothing more than a dreamy murmur, I've never felt so turned on in my whole darn life, especially when the flimsy shorts ride up between her bum cheeks and I can see her buttocks perfectly, rounded and ready.

Now, thank heaven you're only a notebook, Kitten, because what I did next is dreadful. But I promised to tell you everything, so here goes. I part my knees and slip my fingers up between my thighs and rub myself through my lacy knickers as I imagine slapping Janey's bum. Just the thought of her lying across me while I lay right into her, making her eyes brighten as she claws my skirt, crying, 'Yes, yes, yes,' is enough to make me come in mere seconds, arching and groaning as the orgasm swallows me.

As I collapse back, stunned at myself, I hurriedly try to make myself decent, but Janey is still sleeping, thank God. So I sneak away, devastated at what I'm turning into. Tonight I said no to a man who actually wanted to bed me, and came home to assault my twenty-three-year-old tenant.

I'm turning into a pervert. And I need to take action right now.

So upstairs, in my bedroom, I tell myself, 'Never again,' and I vow that, tomorrow, I'll make plans to meet Guy for dinner and this time we'll screw one another. Then I won't think of assaulting Janey Prince again because Guy is a man with a cock – and men with cocks are the only thing I'm into. Really, deep down, I'm a man's kind of girl.

2.30 a.m.

I can't sleep, Kitten. All I want is to touch my poor pussy, thinking of Janey's buttocks. But that's as bad as touching her again without her permission. And I'm not going to do that, I promise, Kitten. This shoe shop manager had a strange, twisted blip, but she's committed to becoming respectable again. And so, Kitten, goodnight.

CHAPTER FOUR

In His Shoes

Wednesday, 7 March

Dear Kitten,

Today was – and still is – grey and rainy. And who buys shoes on a rainy day? Answer: an elderly woman who has a funeral to dress for and shakes her stick when you suggest court heels. I thought elderly people were usually polite, but since I've been working at Pussyfoot I've met all types. So, by the time lunch break came, I was relieved to meet Gladys for lunch at the Spring Onion Café. It's our favourite place because it's never too crowded – plus their baked potatoes are to die for. Turns out, Gladys is making the most of reverting to being a meat-eater by stuffing her face full of sausages, no less. 'You'll starve,' she tells me as I dip into my baked potato. 'You need some extra weight,' she says, glancing at my waistline.

'Just because I'm not a porker like you are,' I say. And we both burst out laughing because we're silly beyond words.

Truth is, Gladys has surpassed herself today. She's wearing a peacock-blue shirt with a topaz pendant and her hair is up in a bun, little tendrils framing her big brown eyes. She smells of expensive scent and she's a bright vision on a rainy day.

Anyway, she soon has me spilling the beans about my date with Guy. As I tell the story she watches me, sipping her tea, the topaz pendant around her neck gleaming away. And even when I get to the bit about kissing Guy goodbye, she only gives a little sideways smirk, because when I'm down about something, Gladys can always tell.

Once I've told her everything – except the bit about fondling my tenant's bum – she reaches across and takes my hands, golden bangles clinking. 'I just thought you'd like a rich guy who worshipped your feet. If he's not for you, he's not for you. But he'll understand, girl. From what I've seen, he's pretty decent.'

'What makes you think I don't like him?' I ask.

Gladys rolls her eyes. 'Energy … tone … blah, blah, blah … Plus you're my mate. I know these things.'

I give a sigh. 'Gladys, I think I'm having a mid-life crisis.'

Gladys snorts. 'Join the effing club. I'm thinking of taking up belly dancing in Madeira and having sex with five oiled Chippendales. Does that sound like non-crisis behaviour?' I grin because I can't help it – Gladys can't fail to make me abandon my cares. 'Seriously,' she says, 'Think about my life.' So I do.

Thing is, Gladys divorced a guy who started beating on her after their son took off to heaven knows where. Sometimes, this son drops her an email. She doesn't think he ever reads her replies. This, I have decided, would be enough to drive any vegetarian back towards meat pies. 'And every time I get a guy home, I go off him,' Gladys says, toying with half a sausage. 'Take Guy. Nice man. Like him a lot. But in bed, he pulls out halfway through – well, halfway through *for me* – and comes all over my shoes, hand jerking away like he's shaking a bottle of ketchup. And I'm not like you, Debs. I like my shoes, but there's a limit.'

I make a face, like I'm appalled – especially since she clearly thinks I'd want this kind of attention! But in truth she isn't wrong because I feel a little turned on. Me and my fricking libido.

'Thank God for my trusty vibe,' she says.

'Your what?'

'Vibrator,' she says. And I have to look at my hands – I've never been so embarrassed. 'You do *have* a sex toy, don't you?' she says. 'A vibe or a dildo? Or a porn vid or two?' And when she sees me shake my head, she says, 'Holy smoke, I can't believe we've never talked about this. No vibrator? Really? I mean, how do you survive?'

Holy punch-bag, Kitten! Suddenly, *any* topic of conversation is better than 'things to stick up your privates' so I decide to trust her and spill the beans about my latest problem. 'Listen, Glads,' I say. 'Can you keep a secret?'

'My lips are sealed,' she says, chewing on some sausage.

'I think … I might have the hots for my tenant.'

Gladys's face lights up. 'You old dog!' she cries, laughing and slamming the table so everything jolts and clanks. Then her brow furrows as the cogs turn. 'Hold on,' she says, 'I thought your tenant was a girl.'

'She is.'

Gladys stops chewing. 'Oh,' she says, putting her fork back down. She looks at me for a while, her head tipped. Then she raises her eyebrows and falls back in her chair. 'Well, is this tenant a lezzie too?'

I nod, trying to ignore the L-word.

'Bull's-eye,' Gladys announces. 'So where's the prob?'

The ease with which she says this takes me aback. 'She's got a girlfriend,' I say.

'Are they serious?' she asks.

I say I don't think so – it looked like they were fighting last night.

Gladys throws up her hands. 'Again I say, where's the prob?'

'Glads, she's twenty-something. It would be like child abuse.'

'Don't be silly. Why d'you think Guy came on to me?

I'm twenty years his senior! Because all the young ones are screwing forty-year-olds these days. We oldies are a fetish. Haven't you heard of cougars?'

'That's a man thing, isn't it?'

Gladys gives another snort. 'Sweetie,' she says, nabbing a forkful of my potato. 'I love you, but you make a very odd queer.'

Back at the store, Pearl calls in with a sore throat. It's me, alone, with nothing to do except stare out at the rain, so when my phone goes off, I'm relieved. Turns out it's Guy. As I answer, I feel lightheaded from this crush of mine, and as soon as I hear his swanky-smooth accent I'm melting on the spot. He asks if I'm busy and, when I say I'm not, he says he'd guessed as much, with this weather. 'I want you to do something for me,' he says, and when I ask what, he tells me he's going to buy me a pair of shoes.

'Hold on,' I say, 'sweet as that is, I can't accept gifts. It doesn't feel right.'

'Well, I'm sure the manager of that lovely store of yours will give you back your money,' he says, 'especially if you decide you can't accept the goods.'

I laugh. He laughs.

'All right,' I say. After all, I could do with a lift.

With that, he makes me walk him around the store, filling him in on the shoes I like. Something in black with heels, he says. Something where you can see a fair amount of foot. 'Think cleavage,' he tells me, 'but the foot variety.'

I'm about to remind him that defining 'cleavage' depends on my knowing which part of my foot is the 'breast', and he gives a sexy, slightly devilish laugh that makes me burn. I walk him through classic stilettos, sparkly wedges, kitten-heel evening sandals, spiky-heeled strappy shoes; and of course, seeing as shoes are some of my favourite items on earth, I get all chirpy and excitable. Soon, we're having a good old naughty chinwag about how five-inch heels do lovely things to the calf, and whether wedge heels can ever be called 'lickable'. I feel turned on and embraced for who I am, all at the same time.

Henry was never interested in my shoes. He wasn't the shoe type. But somehow, I managed to convince myself that this meant *I* wasn't interesting – and suddenly, flirting with Guy, I can see how wrong I was.

He opts for a pair of black pointy slingback stilettos, with silver reflective heels, and makes me model them in front of the mirror. 'Good,' he says, as I strut towards my reflection. 'Now, tell me what you look like.'

My cheeks flush and I check that there aren't any customers. But the shop – in fact the whole darn street – is silent and empty, what with the rain coming down. So what the hell? If this makes me crazily horny, I can always slip round the back of the shop and … you know … go to the bathroom.

(Dear God, Kitten. What a floozy I've become!).

So I describe my legs in their flesh-coloured sheers, the calves pulled taut as I stride. And his voice becomes breathier, heavier, more strained. 'Do your hips … move when you walk?' he asks, making the word 'walk' sound like a controlled explosion. And when I tell him that yes, my hips rock a little in my pencil skirt because of how tight it is, he says, 'I want you to know that I just unzipped. I'm sitting behind my desk, with my personal assistant just outside the door, and I'm jerking at myself like crazy. That's how horny you make me.' He pauses, as pleasure floods to my groin and I'm suddenly hot with arousal and shame. 'Are you turned on?' he asks.

'Yes,' I whisper.

He calls on the Lord then and lets out a groan, before telling me to sit in a chair and run my fingers beneath my skirt before stroking all the way from the top of my thigh down to the bridge of my foot. When I do this, it feels like my hands are his, and my legs tingle beneath my fingertips. I glance up, in case someone is watching. And I'm surprised to find how disappointed I am not to see a voyeur beyond the glass.

'I want to grab your foot,' he tells me, 'and press it onto my cock.'

'Are you hard?' I find myself asking.

'Never been harder,' he says, through a moan.

Oh, God! The mere thought of Guy being hard makes my pussy heat and fill. I feel like grinding my groin against the chair I'm sitting on – grinding and grinding until I come. In fact, just the thought makes me revolve my hips a little and the pleasure is such a relief that I grip the seat of the chair. 'Touch yourself,' he moans.

I'm sorely tempted. 'It wouldn't be professional,' I say.

'That's what makes it fun,' he says. 'God, I'm so close to shooting off.'

And without even thinking, I'm trailing my fingers up my stockings and beneath my skirt again – except this time I hitch my skirt up a little in order to burrow deeper, and there I am, sitting in Pussyfoot Shoes, with my thighs spread and my fingers rubbing my pussy through the gusset of my knickers, softly at first, and then faster, faster.

'That's it,' he says, softly, his voice like a soft roar. 'I can tell you're doing it. Your breathing's changed.'

'Where … are you going to … come?' I gasp, right at the brink of climax.

'Oh, God,' he moans, 'oh, sweet, fucking God.'

'Say it,' I plead, so close to climax that it hurts.

'All over your shoes,' he moans, and then he shouts out, 'All over your fucking feet!' and suddenly he's groaning, out of control, all 'yes' and 'God' and 'holy fuck' and 'sweet Jesus' and 'oh, oh, oh'.

And suddenly, I imagine him walking through the door

and finding me there, with my thighs spread, rubbing my pussy as I stare at him, and he glares at me, all lust and power, and unzips his trousers before grasping his cock and jerking away at it, before stumbling towards me as he comes all over my shoes, covering my stockinged feet in a stream of warm liquid. And suddenly, I'm tipping into an unhinged orgasm that arcs and floods and makes me cry out, grasping the chair with my free hand.

And you know what he says, Kitten, as I sink back, panting and amazed? He says, 'You are the hottest woman to ever have graced a pair of high heels.' And though my whole face flushes, I smile.

7.15 p.m.

I'm on the bus, on my way home, and the weather's still hopeless. Plus my afternoon wasn't exactly a walk in the park. After the sizzling phone sex with Guy, I felt as if I'd tainted the shop. When customers eventually came in, I felt unprofessional, sleazy and corrupt. I was certain I smelled of sex, even though I'd soaped myself down, and my patter wasn't as smooth as normal. Then Guy called me and said he wanted to buy me the shoes I'd worn, and I accepted – not because I felt I should, but because seeing them there, on the central display, kept making my stomach churn. How could I watch another woman trying them on? I'd feel cheap.

8.15 p.m.

So I heated up some soup and had dinner in front of the TV. No sign of Janey. It's times like these when I kind of miss Henry. I mean, there was always a TV show we'd watch together, chat about it a bit, moan about how improbable the whole lousy plot was. That was Henry all over, though – we got on perfectly when we were complaining about someone that wasn't one of us. And of course, Gladys works at the pub on Wednesday evenings – she's only doing the job so she can study half-time in psychology. That's Gladys for you. Intelligent type.

Anyhoo, I started worrying about Janey a little. Going out, God knows where, with a girl like Lil? But how silly! Acting like the girl's mother! (Maybe I need a pet or something. A cat. I'd like a cat.) Still, when I move the magazines out of the way, so I can rest my feet on the coffee table, I notice a battered book with a pic of a platform sandal on the front. It's called *Shoe: A History*. One of Janey's study books, I'm guessing. With my feet up, I lie back, letting the aches drain out of my pins, and I open it to a random page and start to read. 'Yes, limitation was part of the stiletto's original purpose. By essentially binding the foot, the whole walk and stance of the wearer is changed – they are forced to walk in a restricted style, which many found sexy. All the same, an argument can be made for empowerment where restriction is *truly* chosen and eventually overcome. We choose to restrict ourselves when we take on a stronger opponent in order to learn the art of boxing; or when we have a tattoo in order to express ourselves – a piece of art that may never be removed. Women who regularly wear high heels become adept at doing almost anything in them. And of course, considering a stiletto heel can make a fearful weapon, it makes no sense to say that all stiletto wearers are disempowered. In fact, the rise of the dominatrix archetype suggests the very opposite.'

I was so inspired by what I was reading that I didn't notice my phone was ringing. When I answered, it was Gladys. 'I thought you were working tonight,' I said.

'I am, poppet, but I wanted to check in. Make sure you're OK.'

'I'm fine,' I say. In the background, I hear the front door open and slam.

'I didn't mean to make fun of you being a bit gay and all that,' says Gladys. 'Felt awful about it afterwards. I mean, you came out to me – that's a privilege, and I'd hate you to think –'

'Came out!' I cried, horrified. 'I did not come out!'

'Saying, "I have a crush on a woman" is coming out, pet, like it or not.'

I open my mouth to say something, but I have no response, so I close it again, silent. At last, I say, 'I didn't think about it that way. But you're right. And you don't have to apologise, Glads. You were joking around. No harm.'

Gladys gives a sigh of relief. 'Well, good. Anyway, what you up to?'

I tell her I'm reading this amazing book about the politics of the stiletto and she erupts in a fit of laughter. 'Politics! That's zany!'

'What's zany?'

'They're only shoes, love. They're hardly going to start a revolution!'

And she jokes like that for quite a while, until I'm fed up and have to say goodbye. Who made Gladys the bloody queen of academic study? Still embittered, I wander out of the living-room and almost bump into Janey. She's wearing tracky bums and a tight, white T-shirt that says 'Bless the Butch' on the front. In one hand she's holding a pair of green hand weights, and in the other she's carrying some kind of green smoothie that looks depressingly like pondweed. 'I didn't hear you come in,' I say.

'That's me,' she says, all serious. 'Always creeping around.'

Thinking of the way I explored her buttocks while she was sleeping, I guiltily flush. 'Actually,' I say, in an attempt to change the topic, 'I was just perusing your shoe book.'

'Oh, yeah?' she says. She smiles then – it's always so

welcome and unexpected, that sweet, blue-eyed sparkle. 'What did you think?' And she tips her head, so genuinely interested that all of a sudden I'm babbling on about restriction and empowerment, and how I see that all the time at the shop.

'How so?' she asks.

I tell her about my drag queen who came in the other day. You'd never know Billie was a drag queen – stunning woman, she is – but she had a drag contest coming up, like she often does, and needed to look snazzy. 'She says stuff like, "Shoes are the soul of me. Without them, I lack confidence and suddenly I'm worried about what everybody thinks."'

Janey nods. 'Identity,' she says.

'Exactly!' And I'm glowing inside, Kitten, because Janey understands me. Unlike Gladys, she knows that shoes are important.

'Look,' says Janey, shifting her weight and lowering her gaze. 'I'm sorry about Lil the other night. She told me you caught her smoking on the step. I did tell her not to do that, but we'd had a fight.'

'That's OK,' I said. 'Everyone all right, though, love?'

She sighs. 'Oh, it's fine. Love isn't easy, is it?' Her lovely blue eyes look so sad that I reach forward and touch her bare arm, and suddenly my whole arm is tingling with the buzz I feel when our skins connect. 'It *should* be easy for you,' I say. 'Love, I mean.'

She smiles. 'Thanks, Deborah.'

'Call me Debs,' I say.

'Thanks, Debs,' she says. 'You're lovely.'

And that word, *lovely*, stays with me all the way to bed, glowing like an ember in my mind.

12.30 a.m.

Dear God, Kitten! I'm awake. Here's why.

First, Janey's sleeping alone tonight. I know because I couldn't sleep myself, so I decided to go and get Janey's book on shoes from the table, thinking it would help to rest my mind. Anyway, as I'm passing Janey's room, I hear this soft little moan, and I feel it like a burning pulse deep inside my pussy. (Honestly, Kitten! Smutty words are part of my everyday vocab, these days!) There's a line of light surrounding Janey's bedroom door, and when she moans again, more loudly, I'm drawn to her like a magnet. So I do a terrible thing! I kneel down in front of her door, my bare knees on the carpet, and gaze through the keyhole. Janey is lying on the floor, no less, her legs bent and splayed apart as she fucks herself with some kind of object. It's pale-blue and she's thrusting it fast, and oh, my God, I'm completely transfixed. She's wearing the same tight T-shirt I saw her in earlier, but her lower half is bare, and her pussy, which is covered in downy blonde hair, is so wet that I hear the squelch as she pushes the toy in and out. Her phone is at her ear – she's listening to someone – but she isn't saying anything, just thrusting the toy. I find myself rubbing my own pussy as I crouch there, imagining I am in charge of the blue toy, and Janey's eyes are fixed on mine. The heat I feel as I touch myself builds like crazy, and soon I'm dipping right into my pyjama bottoms and fucking my own pussy. I want to cry out myself because it feels so good, and I imagine peeling Janey's T-shirt back and sucking on her breasts as I thrust that toy into her. Janey seems close – her eyes have glazed over, and I can see a spot of drool just at the left of her lips as she rolls and thrusts and pushes the toy in more deeply. Suddenly she murmurs, 'Yes, I'm your slut, your little slut ... yes, right up my ... God ...' and suddenly the phone crashes to the floor and she's groaning and thrusting and crying tiny swear-words. And just when she seems to be coming back down, she's suddenly bucking again, and my own climax takes me over and I'm trying so hard to stay quiet as I feel the hot pleasure shooting through me. When I get back to my bedroom, I'm so turned on that I can barely scramble into my bed. As I touch myself beneath the sheets, I imagine that Janey is fucking me with that toy – the same one she's had in her own pussy – and the sight of her above me, now utterly unclothed, with those tight little breasts and that pale, flawless skin, makes me purr and roll. But soon I want to imagine her body on top of mine, so I grab my pillow and push it between my thighs, rubbing myself against it as I would against her. And suddenly I'm so aroused that the whole room is morphing: the walls are falling back, and in the moonlight the Georgia O'Keeffe lily on the wall slowly expands. And I'm fucking Janey, and she's fucking me – we're rubbing against each other's thighs, the sweet friction unbearable, as I topple into a climax that makes me splay my pussy hard against the pillow, as I ride the crest of this stretched-out high.

Then after, as I lie collapsed and spread, I remember how Janey embraced my interest in shoes. Feeling suddenly aglow, I get up, flick on the light and wander over to my wardrobe. Opening the door, I stare down at the dozens of shoes that I adore – my bottle-green slingbacks; my strappy silver wedges; my Dorothy Ruby Slippers; my many pairs of kitten heels and stilettos for every occasion – and I feel sure, as I stand there, gazing down at my collection, that these are somehow an expression of me. I think about the drag queen too, in her yellow dress with her dark skin and her black hair piled up high on her head, and the way she told me, 'I do drag, dear. And when I'm in a pair of heels, there's no one more woman than me.' If shoes make us feel sexy and proud, then surely shoes are important. And maybe they're not much to Glads, but they mean a lot to me.

After all, Kitten, what's more important than the way we feel inside?

CHAPTER FIVE

Bang Goes My Saturday Girl

Saturday, 10 March

Dear Kitten,

I'm too wiped to say more than this: I had to fire Cheryl today. Bang goes my Saturday girl. She was in tears, begged me not to do it, but I'm a businesswoman, Kitten, and she left me no choice. She actually laughed – yes, laughed! – at a woman who was trying on shoes because apparently the pair of leopard-print mules made her look 'like a platypus'. This is what the poor woman told me. And when I talked with Cheryl, she didn't deny it. I had to call in to head office who, it turns out, couldn't have been less interested. So there's a new ad in the paper and more work for yours truly. I was meant to go out for dinner with Guy, but I'm going to cancel and go home to bed.

Sunday, 11 March
10.15 a.m.

Good morning, Kitten,

I woke this morning to the sound of church bells – a reminder that I don't go to church like I'm meant to. My mother, God love her, would scream her head off if she knew I didn't go to Mass every week. Anyway, maybe this lapsed Catholic guilt is what makes me restless while the church bells are ringing – so much so that I have to get up. So the first thing I saw today when I pulled back the curtains was the sunlit back patio with the garden chairs and table pulled back, and Janey Prince doing yoga on a purple mat, in the skimpiest pair of exercise shorts I've ever seen. And every time she folds her torso downwards, touching the ground, or walks her hands forward, keeping her bum in the air, I get a glimpse of those wonderfully tight buttocks, smooth as eggshells in the morning sun. After a few minutes, she looks up and sees me watching, so I throw open the window and offer her some juice, making it look like that was my plan. 'No, I'm good,' she calls. 'You should come out here. It's gorgeous.' And her body language is all warm and open, so I take her up on the offer. Well, why not? Landlord–tenant bonding, and that.

It doesn't take long before I'm making her a smoothie, and blending bananas, yoghurt and apple juice, which I end up delivering to the garden. 'That's so nice of you,' she says, serious as ever, as she rises up from her sun salutation, but when I sit at the side of the garden and place my glass on the table, Janey comes and joins me. We get to talking about shoes, of course. I tell her about the tiger-print stilettos I'm saving up for, and she watches me closely, asking question after question: What makes them so special? When would I wear them? Would I ever use them in the bedroom?

'In the bedroom?' I ask, flushing. 'Well, yes, I suppose I would.'

Janey sighs, leaning back, taking a sip of her smoothie. 'Good for you,' she says. 'I love shoes in the bedroom.' Then she adds, 'I'd love to work in a shoe shop. It'd be like seeing my dissertation in action.' She gives a sigh. 'Either way, I should get a job. Stop draining Mum and Dad's money. It's savings, you know.'

A switch inside me flicks on. 'Well, are you interested in a job?' I ask.

She sits up straight, eyes open, like a meerkat. 'A job at Pussyfoot?'

'That's right,' I say, 'I need a Saturday girl, and pronto.' She watches me, blue eyes growing large, as I fill her in on the job and pay, and as soon as I've got to the end of my spiel she says, 'It sounds perfect. I can't start this Saturday because I've got an appointment, but I can the week after. How should I apply?'

I tell her she doesn't have to apply. 'Give it a trial period,' I tell her. 'A couple of weeks with full pay, and if it doesn't work out, no spilt milk.'

Janey watches me for a moment, eyes slant in the sunlight, before we shake on it. 'It's like a miracle,' she tells me. 'Like this was meant to happen.'

And I feel a strange tingling inside.

CHAPTER SIX

Meaningful Stilettos

Monday, 12 March

Well, my goodness, Kitten, what a day! First, old Gladys pops in holding a small purple bag – the type you get from a gift store – that matches her stunning silk blouse. She's sorry, she tells me, about what she said the other day. 'Belittled your passion, I did.' She shakes her head. 'What a haggard old bitch I am.'

'Look, I know shoes aren't deep like psychology,' I grumble, and I have to bite my lip to stop myself saying, *Actually shoes are all about psychology.*

Glads shakes her head. 'I was a pig about it, lovey. And given the choice between Freud and some Karen Millen slingbacks, it wouldn't be the doc who'd get my cash.' Glads explains that when she was a kid, she was always pushed to be top of the class. She was the only girl, so she had to keep up with her brothers, who were told they had to be surgeons or psychiatrists and such. 'I liked art best,' she tells me, 'but my parents didn't care when I got good marks for my painting. "Who cares about paint?" they'd ask. It was horrible, really. And now, here I am, doing the same darn thing to you.'

'Forgiven,' I tell her, giving her a hug. And when we're done with the hugging, she hands me the purple bag. 'A make-up pressie,' she says, but when I try to take the bag, she grabs my hand for a second and with big, excitable eyes whispers, 'Open it alone.'

So I stashed it behind the counter, Kitten, but we had a run of customers, and Tanya, whose shift starts at twelve, only just arrived. So now, all intrigued, I get a minute to pop to the loo, and that's where I dip down into the bag and pull out a purple gift box. On the lid of the box, in silver swirly print, are the words *Pandora's Box: Erotic Boutique for Women*.

I catch my breath, Kitten! I know exactly what this is!

Sure enough, inside the box, lodged in a silky layer, is a small, black, bullet-shaped vibrator. When I take it out and press the tiny button at the end it purrs and hums in my palm, and when I hold it against my skirt so that it vibrates through the fabric, it feels so good that I let out an instant moan. In a matter of moments, I've dialled Guy's number and we're dirty talking. 'I'm on my knees, jerking off,' he growls, 'and you're in those perfect shoes ...'

'Describe them,' I say, slipping the buzzing thing up my skirt and between my thighs, where it feels deliciously good.

And do you know, Kitten, he *does* describe them, feature by feature. The platform sole, the stiletto heels, the cherry-coloured suede and the stockings I was wearing. Henry would never have been able to describe my shoes from memory! But soon Guy's back to the fantasy, reminding me how I raised my skirt and touched my pussy in front of him. So I press the buzzing plastic hard against my briefs, letting my pussy drink up all the wonderful vibrations, and I find myself grinding against the purring toy, letting out a moan as I fall back against the tiling. 'I'm gonna come all over your shoes,' cries Guy, 'all over your fucking shoes.' And in my head I can see him doing just that, and I push the buzzing bullet right inside my briefs, against my slippery sex. Again I moan, but more loudly now, and I'm pushing the bullet inside myself, unable to stop as I grind against its pulsing. 'Oh, God,' I cry out as I begin to feel the heat of my climax, and suddenly Guy's moaning, 'All over your shoes, yes, all over them!' and I fill with a perfect pleasure that makes me buck in spite of myself as I slide down those tiles, coming again and again and again, until I'm utterly spent, with my bum on the floor.

I feel dirty. And cheap. Like I've ruined sacred ground. That's twice I've come in Pussyfoot Shoes. What kind of manager does that make me?

'You're one hell of a woman,' breathes Guy. 'I'm gonna shower you in gifts.'

'That orgasm was gift enough,' I tell him. 'Have to rush. Bye for now.'

Then I pull myself to my feet, clean myself up, and exit the bathroom hoping no one heard my moans.

As if the store is punishing me, Pearl and I have a spate of bad luck. One woman brings back some Gucci heels that cost several hundred pounds, saying the strap snapped the first time she wore them. She seems sincere enough, so I sigh and give her a refund. Then, to top it all off, I spend an hour – a whole hour, dammit – trying to convince a buxom woman that her feet are extra-wide and can she please stop trying on the expensive shoes because she is stretching them. Eventually, she leaves in a fit, dabbing her eyes. 'There's nothing wrong with having big feet,' I call as she goes. Pearl gives me one hell of a look, in response. 'What?' I say. 'It's the truth!'

'Some people,' say Pearl, blowing hot air onto her glasses, 'can't cope with the truth. But we do like customers who don't slam us online,' she mumbles.

And what can I say to that? Pearl is right, as flipping usual. It's hard living with someone ten years your junior who looks like a blonde Jessica Rabbit in preppy glasses, has a brain like a razor and isn't afraid of speaking her mind.

But Pearl's OK really. It's me that's a mess.

Anyway, things improve when I return from coffee break. Pearl produces a shoebox from behind the counter. 'A rather dashing man popped in while you were gone,' she says, with a wink. 'He bought you these and told me to keep them for you.'

I lift the lid from the box, and my heart does a backflip. Guy's only gone and bought me the tiger-print stilettos! I run my hand along the velvety uppers, the strappy backs and peep toes. I've handled these shoes so often, Kitten, longing for the day when I could take them away! And there they are, in my hands.

'Gucci, no less,' gushes Pearl. 'Go on then! Try 'em on!'

So I do. And I feel like a princess as I strut up and down the shop, my new shoes sinking into the carpet. 'How do I look?' I ask Pearl.

She claps her hands. 'They're perfect! They make you walk like a tiger. You should call him.'

'But I'm only just back from coffee break!'

Pearl flaps the air. 'Do you see a swarm of customers?' And when I shake my head she says, 'Well, then.'

So this time I'm up in the kitchen while Guy orders me about. 'Have you got them on?' he growls.

I say I have, and he starts telling me how much he wants to come on them. And again I'm touching my poor wet pussy beneath the staff table, pushing myself to climax as he moans in my ear.

But you know, Kitten, while I'm fucking myself, it's Janey I'm really thinking about. Janey has a cock this time. No, really. A cock. And I'm back in that hallway, modelling the shoes for her – the cherry platform stilettos – only this time, when she crouches down to look more closely at my feet, I raise my left foot and place it in her lap, resting the heel lightly just above her knee. She's transfixed as she runs her hands up and down my legs. 'Deborah, you're gorgeous,' she says. And that's when I see the bulge inside her jeans. She looks up at me, and I'm so turned on I could burst. Still holding my stare, she rubs her hands over my shoe, running a finger up and down the stiletto heel, before pulling her jeans open and taking her cock in her hand. She stares up at me, fiercely, as if she could tear me to pieces, and murmurs, 'I'm going to come all over them, Deborah,' and when she says my name, I climax.

Oh, God, how I climax!

On the other end of the line, Guy says, 'You're too hot to handle.'

And I say, 'Guy, I've got to go.'

And he says, 'Talk to you later, baby.'

And frankly, Kitten, I feel like a piece of shit, having phone sex with him while I dream about my super-young tenant. So I return to Pearl, who's got nothing to do, and she says, 'Well?'

'I told him how much I adore them,' I say, but I glance

down at the shoes, which are suddenly less glamorous than I remembered. 'Think I'll change 'em though,' I tell Pearl. 'Keep them nice.'

But sadly, I wonder if they'll ever seem nice again.

7.45 p.m.

Oh, now I really have seen it all! But I'll start at the beginning.

I got home half an hour ago and I'm in an awful mood. The place smells of incense and there's a droning music coming from upstairs. One of those goth bands or something. So I march on up, thinking I'll ask Janey to turn it down, when I see that the bedroom door is ajar. 'Janey?' I call, as I reach the top of the stairs. 'D'you mind if I close the door?'

And a plaintive voice says, 'Um ... Deborah, I need some help.'

I pause at the door. Something tells me this is going to be weird. And when I step into her room, it turns out I wasn't wrong! Kitten, the girl is splayed on her double bed in a grey bra and matching briefs (so scant, Kitten, they're barely there at all), and she's spread-eagled across the bed, with each of her wrists bound to the bed knobs of my Auntie Doris's antique queen-size. Her breasts swell more than I thought they would, and I can see the shapes of her nipples through the grey Lycra, and her belly and thighs are delightfully pale, and there are tiny specks of freckles round her cleavage. She's so stunning that I stare at her for far too long. 'Sorry,' she says, at last, with a sigh. 'This is so fucking embarrassing.' Then she tells me that she and Lil had a fight. 'Let's just say, once she'd tied me up, she decided to ask me a few tough questions.'

Suddenly, the truth hits me. 'She didn't *leave* you like this?' I ask.

'Looks like it,' says Janey. 'Never get all truthy when your lover's got you trussed.'

This makes me want to laugh – and hard – but I bite my lip. But Janey catches the glint in my eye, and suddenly we're both giggling away. In fact, after a minute, our laughter gets so raucous that I have to lean against the pine chest of drawers, Kitten, to keep my balance. (Never was one for yoga, you know.) And poor Janey's got tears running down her face, God bless her, so I go over and wipe them away with the pad of my thumb, and we watch each other for a moment, and I think, Dear God, you're beautiful, with that haunting face and those blue-blue eyes – 'fuck-me blue' as Glads would say – and your wonderful body, so sleek and unspoiled. And suddenly, things get awkward, so I offer to help and soon I'm picking my way round the clothes on the floor, trying to find the key that Lil apparently threw on the floor when she left.

As I release poor Janey, she says, 'Learning point: only submit with someone you trust.'

'Are you saying you don't trust Lil?'

Janey's eyebrows rise. 'Would *you* trust Lil in the bedroom right now?'

'Well, at least she hasn't been unfaithful,' I say.

Janey, who's now free and rubbing her wrists, gives me a you're-plain-crazy kind of look. 'I'd call locking up your girl and tossing the key pretty damn unfaithful. Especially when she's telling you the truth. And if Lil *had* ever screwed someone behind my back, you'd have just said something pretty fucking tactless.'

Oh, Kitten, I cover my eyes! Janey's right! I'm a wreck! Tactless as they come. 'I'm so sorry,' I say. 'I'm so full of tripe that I'd sink a ship.' Then I sit on the bed, facing away from Janey, staring into my palms. I should say something more, but I don't know what. Why do I feel so lost of all a sudden, as if everything's wrong, as if I'm useless? The tears start to come. Is this what it's like to be sexually in tune, Kitten? Is this what life does to you when you start to feel sexually free? I feel Janey's hand on my shoulder – warm and firm – and she says, 'Are you worried that Guy isn't faithful?'

'Not really,' I say. 'It's more to do with my ex.'

She squeezes my shoulder so sweetly that little sparks seem to shoot down my arm. Then she crawls round the back of me and begins to massage my shoulders. Oh, my, her pressure feels wonderful. 'Tell me about this ex,' she says. So I do. I start at the beginning. All those years spent making myself look sexy, hoping that Henry, with his steady brown gaze and delectable hands, would scoop me up in his arms and take me to bed. I tell Janey how many times I made him lovely meals at the end of my work day, even though I was tired and he never made meals for me. And then I tell her how Henry stopped meeting my eyes when he spoke, how he started working later and later, how when I asked his advice about how I looked, he'd say, 'Always great,' but wouldn't even take the time to scan me.

And when I tell Janey how I followed him in my car and saw him with the woman in the raincoat and bowler hat, and how the woman turned me on, and how Henry had never looked at me that way, I feel Janey's arms slipping around me, as she presses her cheek to my cheek. I can feel her breasts rubbing against my shoulder blade, and do I imagine it, Kitten, or is it true that I can feel her hard nipples, rubbing against my back? She whispers, 'I know it's a cliché, but you're better off without him,' and I can't do anything but nod because I'm drunk on her closeness, the scent of her coconut soap, the warmth of her breath. Then she says, 'And you'd never have known who you were if you hadn't seen him like that.'

'What do you mean?' I ask.

Janey says, 'People go through their whole lives without discovering who they are. And when you discover your own sexuality, everything else kind of falls into place.'

Returning to my shoulder massage, she says she used to think she was straight, except part of her knew she wasn't. She'd watch heterosexual porn, she explains – the mere mention of this makes me flush – when really she'd only be interested in the woman. She had no success with boys, so she thought she was a freak. 'But I wasn't a freak. I just wasn't accepting myself ... so how could anyone else even begin to accept me?'

I tell her that isn't what I'm like. 'I'm just obsessed with sex,' I say, feeling the tears returning. 'I just want to think about sex, and have sex.'

'Of course you do,' says Janey. 'You're a flesh-and-blood human being who wants to feel alive.'

Janey begins to massage my scalp, and I close my eyes – so this is how it feels to have her hands in my hair. She uses a perfect pressure and has a surprisingly sensual touch. Dear God, Kitten, I feel dizzy with desire. 'Do you journal?' she says.

I gawp at her. 'Yes, actually, I do.'

'Well, when I first realised I was into women, I journalled. I was like you, back then. I mean, changing your whole life because of your sexuality can feel weird because society hates sex. But if you journal, you'll start to see that sex can be the root of happiness. You'll love the people you want to love, in the ways you want to love them.'

'You mean, I'll screw the people I want to screw?'

'You're not listening, Debs. I said *the people you want to love*. This is just as much about love as it is about flesh.'

Well, I'm not sure I quite believe her, Kitten. Young people sometimes seem so confident, don't they? But it doesn't sound like she's telling a lie and my gut tells me to go with this. I have to say, I appreciate Janey more than words can say, right now. She's so sincere, so thoughtful. I wish Lil would treat her well.

So I thank her warmly and give her a hug, even though she's in her underwear. And then I say, 'I should go and have some dinner. Have you eaten?'

She nods, so I turn to go.

'Deborah,' she says, and I turn. 'Have you seen my display?' She's pointing at the opposite wall, and suddenly my eyes are opened. She's hung a huge pinboard and covered it with pictures and clippings of shoes. 'It's amazing,' I gasp, as I rush over. It's an explosion of colours and shapes. There are crazy platforms, old-fashioned loafers, ballet shoes for ballerinas, high heels of all shapes and sizes, red shoes, black shoes, rainbow-coloured shoes, celebrities like Marilyn Monroe and some goth woman in the pointiest boots you've ever seen … shoes, shoes, shoes. And the sight of them makes me laugh out loud. 'It's fantastic!' I say, clapping my hands together. 'What fun!'

And when I turn to her, she's beaming. 'I knew you'd

get it,' she told me. 'When you love a thing, you love a thing.'

'Yes,' I say, and we hold one another's gazes for a while, and I feel like I might cry again – but in a better way.

And now, half an hour later, I'm down in the kitchen, tucking into my Lean Cuisine, wearing my new tiger-print stilettos. I don't know what I feel about them right now. They feel stolen, almost, or like a gift with added baggage. But they're beautiful objects. And as Janey says, there's nothing wrong with that.

CHAPTER SEVEN

His and Hers

Tuesday, 13 March
11.15 a.m.

Dear Kitten,

I haven't got long to write to you today because I'm
going to Guy's place this evening. He's cooking for me,
Kitten! I think we're going to bond some more like we
did on the phone ... and sex in the bedroom is a whole
lot more intimate than fucking ourselves in a field. Also,
I've had two phone conversations in which Guy hasn't
mentioned phone sex even once. He's asked me how
my day was, and filled me in about a business trip he's
taking in a couple of weeks' time. There's something
special about talking just for the sake of talking. I think
he wants to take things to the next level. Romantically,
I mean.

10.45 p.m.

Oh, Kitten, as I write, Guy is asleep at my side, his tanned chest rising and falling, the white sheets twisted round his waist. He's a very sexy man, Kitten. A real catch. So why do I feel just a little bit empty?

Anyway, when I arrived in a taxi he insisted on paying for, he was right in the middle of creating a lovely meal. Ricotta-stuffed ravioli with home-made tomato sauce, topped with fresh Parmesan and a side salad. For dessert: a pile of strawberries with dark chocolate truffles – he fed these to me on the sofa, as I lounged against him, his breath all close and chocolatey, his eyes a sparkling brown. For every strawberry, he told me I had to kiss him. 'That's the cost,' he teased. And sure enough, I laid each of these kisses along that manly jaw line, enjoying the scent of his aftershave and the smoothness of his just-shaved cheek.

This is where we discussed our star signs. I told him I was Sagittarius and it turns out he's Aries – we're meant to be a perfect match! 'You're a go-getter,' I told him.

He gave a soft laugh. 'That's true. And what about you, Madame Archer?' He laid a chocolate on my tongue and I felt it dissolve, oh, so sweetly.

So I give him the low-down on Sagittarians. First, I tell him, we seem very fiery and outgoing, but we're actually quite sensitive deep down. I also tell him we tend to talk a lot, and sometimes we're loudmouths – can't always keep a secret. 'At the same time, we're incredibly perceptive. We have a habit of hitting the nail on the head when it comes to getting to the root of things.'

'A bit of a psychologist,' he says, 'like Gladys.'

'In my way,' I say. 'But we're also wanderers. We like our freedom.'

His eyes brighten. 'Yes, I can see that in you! You're adventurous. Like your choice in shoes.'

I stretched out my foot to stare at the tiger-print stilettos, which, I might add, were looking stunning, teamed with flesh-toned stockings and my fitted black dress with the lacy trim. I could see his gaze lingering, so I lowered my foot – I didn't want to destroy this moment. 'I'm a freethinker, too.'

'You don't say!' he says with a smile and a sideways look.

I slap his arm.

And with that I'm sinking beneath his weight like some 50s starlet, and his hard on is pressing down on my belly, and my hands are exploring his wonderful backside. 'I haven't undressed you yet,' I murmur, when he comes up for air.

With a slick grin, he undoes his belt and swishes it from his jeans so it hangs from his hand like a whip.

I laugh. 'Careful, cowboy.'

He drops the belt to the floor. And soon he's unzipping

the back of my dress, and laying damp little kisses down the side of my neck, and I unbutton his shirt, and I slide off his jeans, and I straddle him in his boxers as he wrestles me out of my bra. He insists that I keep my shoes and stockings on, and I have to admit, I'm relieved by this – I love to have him worshipping my shoes. Besides, he's mad about my legs and feet, and can't stop running his fingers over my glossy stocking-tops. 'What shall we start with?' he asks, as I sit astride him.

I tell him I'd like to do it just like this. Me in his lap; riding up and down. He agrees – and it's stupid, I know, but I'm so proud that I've brought the condom that I'm feeling rosy-cheeked as I slide it onto him. And oh, when he clasps my hips and pulls me right onto him, I feel him filling every inch of me. I also realise that this was how Henry took the bowler-hatted girl ... while I was watching at the window ... and I can't help imagining Janey sitting beneath me with a wonderful black silicone toy. Oh, my! I'm so wet as I fantasise, my hips working harder, my breath coming in starts, that he feels like he's slicked with oil. And he must be a mind-reader because, once I'm close to climax, he whispers, 'If there was someone else here, Deborah, would it be a man or a woman?'

And I say, 'Guess!'

And he says, 'A woman.'

So I blurt out something – I don't know what – because

mentioning Janey makes me hornier than ever. And my breasts are suddenly Janey's breasts as I rub and pinch the nipples, and she's there, beneath me, groaning, gasping and crying, 'Deborah, baby ...' And that's when I come too, riding Guy, my hips lunging by themselves, because they're faster and more desperate than my poor befuddled mind. And it's as if a wild light is filling every cell of me: I'm firelit and crazy for what seems like an age.

When I flop on top of him, mumbling, 'You haven't come yet, have you?' Guy says, 'No, angel, but I won't take long.' Then he makes me lie along the couch, while he kneels above me, holding my ankle, pulling my shoe against him, my stiletto heel pressing into his balls, while he fucks my shoe – yes, fucks my shoe – yanking it against himself, before coming in an impressive surge that spurts and showers and spatters my body. And he keeps crying, 'Fucking your ... fucking your ... shoes' right to the very last surge.

It doesn't feel very intimate, Kitten. He's interested in my feet, really. I didn't see him look up once. But guys are afraid of that sort of thing – you know, intimacy, closeness, bonding, right? And afterwards, he lies on top of me and whispers in my ear, 'I come so hard with you. So fucking hard. You're one hell of a woman. Christ, I'm a lucky boy.'

So here I am now, up in his bed, because he insisted that I stay. And we showered together and he kissed me good night, all sparkly and sweet. But by the time I'd managed to clean the semen off my shoes, he was on his back and snoring. Well, I can't say I blame him.

And I don't suppose it matters, Kitten, but I kind of had sex with Janey tonight. I was both with Guy and *not* with Guy. So is that me being the *real, sexual me*? Or is that me just hiding? And what if it's a bit of both?

CHAPTER EIGHT

Scratch 'n Sniff Stilettos

Wednesday, 14 March
7 a.m.

Dear Kitten,
This morning, Guy was different. He's clearly not a morning person. I tried to seduce him by rubbing up against him and biting his ear, but he brushed me off, saying he couldn't. I was horny as hell, and during Guy's shower – which, by the way, he didn't invite me into – I considered digging through my bag for my vibrator, but thought better of it. Instead, I peered through the bathroom door and offered to make him a fry-up, which he turned down straightaway, saying he hadn't got time for breakfast. 'Make a fry-up for yourself if you like,' he called, and he reminded me that the front door locks itself when it closes. He gave me the merest peck on the

cheek on his way out. But he did say he had a surprise for me next week, if I was interested. 'A special something for dinner, next Wednesday,' he murmured. 'I'll confirm with you later today.' And then, as he pulled away, he sparkled like the Guy I know, and added, 'This'll be a real treat for you, Deborah.'

So I guess things are fine after all.

Anyhoo. Today's my day off, Kitten, so I'm meeting up with Glads around eleven. But before that I'm going to eat a proper breakfast. So I rifle round his beautiful kitchen, which has a stainless-steel oven that looks as if Jamie Oliver has crawled all over it and licked it to a shine. Plus Guy has the whitest kitchen cupboards with classy little silver knobs.

On the hunt for food, the most interesting thing I find is pancake mix, *a la* U.S.A. So I follow the instructions on the box and make myself a set of real American pancakes. They're rather tasty, if I say so myself, especially when drizzled with lemon and a coating of brown sugar. Unfortunately, the only tea he has is Twinings. I, dear Kitten, am a P.G. girl.

2.15 p.m.

Meeting up with Glads for coffee was a pleasure, as usual, and she even bought me a Danish pastry to make up for being a twerp. The only thing she asked me about the vibrator was, 'Did the gift work out fine, Miss Scarlet?' before giving an enormous wink. And I said it was just dandy, thank you very much. (Interesting how I flush again all meekly, while I'm wearing sperm-flavoured scratch-and-sniff stilettos, courtesy of Guy and his little explosion.)

Turns out that things at Academic Central aren't so rosy right now for Gladys. She got low marks on a Freud essay because she tore the man to bits without discussing his good points. 'That idiot,' says Glads. 'As if women envy penises!'

'Maybe some of them do,' I say, picturing Janey looking delicious in a strap-on.

'Maybe the Tooth Fairy exists,' says Glads, 'but we don't write essays about *that*, now, do we?'

I'm about to say that there must be men who envy vaginas, but then I remember what she said about her parents wanting her to always get A grades, and I suddenly realise this is Glads being defensive. So I say, 'You tell 'em, Glads,' and she nods, and we're just fine.

Apparently, Gladys has a date with a man who is doing her psychology course. A suave Italian called Marco. He's around the same age as she is. (Wonders may never cease!) 'He's so good at psychology,' she says, her eyes going moony.

'Will he critique Doctor Freud in the sack?' I ask.

And she snorts. So I do too. In fact, we're snorting away for a good long while.

But when she asks why I look so glam and I explain that I stayed at Guy's last night, Glads isn't so perky. 'I thought you were into your tenant?' she says. And when I remind her that Janey is taken, she narrows her eyes as if she can't see me right. 'But you're a dyke, correct?'

Oh, my gosh. What does 'dyke' mean, Kitten? Lesbian? A certain *kind* of lesbian? P.C. or not P.C.? 'I think I might be into women *and* men,' I say.

'Oh.' She takes a sip of her coffee, but she's still watching me all the way through. 'Listen, love,' she says. 'I wouldn't get sweet on the man. He's a bit of fun, don't you think? A bauble. He'll wine and dine a girl, then lay her. Simple.'

'There's nothing wrong with a little romance.'

Gladys puts her hand over mine and her eyes go deep and kind. 'Sweetie, as long as you don't get hurt, OK? Not after Henry. It's your first crush since the split.'

The way she looks at me reminds me of the first time I told her what Henry had been up to. She was the first person who heard me say the words 'Henry's having an affair.' In fact, I broke the news in this very coffee shop, two tables to the left of where we're sitting right now. What was even sadder was the total surprise on her face at the time. 'No way,' she said, reaching across the table. 'Henry's crazy about you.' And I could see why she'd think that. I mean, even though Henry and I didn't have sex, just a few months before I caught him he was buying me flowers every weekend and making me breakfast on Sunday mornings. He'd sit on the bed in his stripy pyjamas, all stubbly, with his greying hair tousled, and he'd take my hands between his own and say, 'The menu today, Lady Deborah, is ...' and he'd reel off the very things we had in the kitchen. He'd offer a 'great British fry-up' or 'croissants with jam' or 'a bacon buttie' or 'Scotch pancakes' and it always made me happy to sit and read a mag while he clanked around in the kitchen downstairs, whistling Louis Armstrong's 'Jeepers, Creepers' or 'Hello, Dolly!' He liked his jazz, did Henry.

But I don't want you to think I was sweet on an arsehole, Kitten. He was only like that towards the end. In fact, he could be extremely romantic. Take our anniversary, for instance, when he always bought me lilies – there were lilies in my wedding bouquet, see, almost twenty years ago now, and not a year went by when I didn't receive an armful on 30 September. That's how romantic Henry could be.

All those years, Kitten. I miss him. My Henry.

Gladys pulls her hand away from mine. 'And anyway,' she adds, 'I'd like to see you dating that Janey. Or some other girl. Why not experiment a bit?'

I don't know what to say about that, so we move on to Gladys's hot date for tomorrow night – this new forty-something Italian with a flashy red sports car. Apparently, he's taking her to see a movie, at the artsy picture house on Remington Ave. It'll probably be some suave international movie. The kind that has subtitles. I hate subtitles. I like to gaze into the faces of the characters and forget to think about anything else.

But Glads says that's because I'm an old romantic.

'You get too attached,' she says. And she's probably right, because, as soon as she says it, I find myself thinking of Guy when he says, 'You are the most beautiful woman to grace a pair of heels.'

'I'm going out with Guy again next week,' I say. 'We're going to dinner. He's bringing me a gift – a surprise, he says.'

Gladys gives a hefty sigh and stretches her lips, like she's totally unimpressed. 'A bottle of lube and a condom, perhaps?'

I can't help but feel she's raining on my parade.

'I'm sorry, sweetie,' she says, taking my hands. 'I know he's very fond of you. But he's a plaything, yes? A hot bit of hot totty.'

And I admit, she's probably right.

9.15 p.m.

My dear Kitten, oh, wait until you hear this!

I get home at around seven. My God, I'm tired. Janey and Lil, who have obviously made up, are in the living-room snogging. Now, when I say snogging, I don't mean a gentle smooch. Lil is lying back in my white leather armchair, with her slender, tanned thighs half-wrapped around Janey's waist. She's wearing a lacy, pink bra and a pair of tan high-heeled shoes. Now, something about these shoes makes me a little angry. (Well, to be honest, Kitten, I'm jealous. Not only are the pair of them getting it on like rabbits, but Lil's clearly given in to Janey's penchant for heels, which means I'm no longer the only Goddess of Stilettos.) But even though I'm fuming, I gaze at them, aroused. Their kissing is carnal – it goes on and on – and though Janey is wearing the tiniest pair of Lycra shorts, Lil manages to push her fingers inside them, letting out a little moan of approval as she strokes those beautiful buttocks. Oh, God, I remember fondling them, Kitten! So soft, so pale, so flawless. And I remember how hard I came ...

Lil peels off her own top, and I get a quick glimpse of her breasts – fairly big, maybe a 34C, with large, plum-coloured nipples, and I admit they're lovely. But it's Janey's breasts I'm longing to see. Then, at last, when Lil peels off Janey's top, there isn't a bra, Kitten! Just a pair of pale, delicious breasts that I only catch for a moment when Janey turns a little and pushes Lil's hair from her face. But oh, my, Kitten, what a gorgeous being this Janey is. Her nipples are small and rosy, and her breasts are tight and perfect, and the way Lil is pawing them makes me fume. What right does she have to fondle my tenant's nipples?

Mind you, seeing as I'm She-Who-Cannot-Be-Trusted-With-Buttocks, I had no right even thinking of this. What a messed-up woman I am.

Still. I go upstairs to take a shower, and on my way back down in my new black jeans and sparkly grey flip-flops, I pause halfway. I can see the girls through the open door. Lil is kneeling on the floor with her head between Janey's thighs, and Janey is lying back, her fingers tangled in Lil's hair. She keeps arching, and moaning, and arching, and moaning, and she's whispering things that I just can't hear, and the look on her face – it's pure rapture, Kitten. Her eyelids are fluttering and her jaw drops, and her whole body tenses, time and again. I have to admit, when Lil leans towards Janey's beautiful nipples and sucks – and maybe bites – them to her heart's content, I imagine I'm her, for a moment, and I'm instantly in a lather. Then suddenly, Lil dips back to Janey's pussy, and Janey arches back, more tense than before, and she murmurs, 'Oh Christ … Christ … Christ,' each word a little louder than the last, before thrusting her hips even harder, so her pussy presses into Lil's open mouth, and crying out in bliss, her whole face contorted with the kind of joy I, for one, would like a little more of.

I sidle away towards the kitchen where I clank the washing-up around until I hear Janey behind me. She's dressed in her little shorts and a tight grey T-shirt. Her nipples are erect underneath. Her face is flushed red, and she smells of beer. 'Oh, God,' she gasps, 'Deborah, I'm so, so sorry.' She's lisping a little – that's when I realise she's drunk.

'You do pay for a *bedroom*,' I snap, clanging a saucer onto the draining rack.

'I didn't know you were home. You're earlier than usual.' ('Usual' sounds like 'you-shoo-all'. That's how tipsy she is).

'Are you saying that if I'm out,' I ask, 'it's fine if you get your ... juices ... on my white leather armchair?'

Janey slurs that it was a spur-of-the-moment thing. She and Lil were making up. She assures me that the armchair is fine – there wasn't anything to clean.

'That's not the point,' I say. 'I shouldn't feel uncomfortable in my own home.'

There's a long pause, followed by some shuffling. 'Oh, my God, you're right, I'm so sorry! I'm a bit drunk. No excuse, though.'

I dunk a mug into the water and scrub it, superhard. 'I noticed Lil was wearing high heels,' I mutter.

Holy mole trap, Kitten, I sound like fifteen years old. Then I notice my mistake. I must have been watching quite carefully to notice Lil's stilettos. But as I carry on scrubbing the dishes, I hear Janey walking towards me, till she's right up close, with her breath on my neck. I feel her warm fingers touching my arms as she says, 'I'm sorry. That was bad form, Deborah. I'll never do it again.'

'Can I trust you, Janey?' I ask. 'Because we'll be working together soon.'

She touches my arm again. 'You can, I swear.' Then, as I turn away, she murmurs, 'No one looks as hot as you in a pair of heels.'

I look back, astonished, as she pushes a lock of hair from my face. 'You're stunning,' she says, softly. 'If only I was twenty years older ...' Then she flushes and glances down at her hands. I can't actually believe what she just said, which is why it takes me a minute to change the topic. (Janey wants *me*? Janey wishes she was *older*?) And as I start to ask her about her project on heels, I notice the heat of arousal trickling down my spine, eventually pooling deep inside me.

By the time I tune into what Janey is saying, she's filling me in on the history of heels. Apparently Napoleon banned high heels in France in an attempt to create equality. 'I don't understand,' I tell her. 'Were high heels fancy or something?'

Janey nods. 'Exactly. For men as well as women. They were a sign of class.'

'And what if you weren't classy?'

'You went barefoot.'

I give a little snort. 'Times haven't changed, then.'

Janey giggles. I giggle.

Oh, Kitten, she's adorable when she laughs.

Suddenly, there's the sound of a door opening upstairs, and Lil is shouting, 'Janey, it's starting! Are you coming?'

Janey gives me an apologetic shrug as she begins to walk away, but then, at the last minute, she turns back again. 'Marie Antoinette went to the gallows in high heels,' she tells me, 'in spite of Napoleon's law.'

'I like a woman who can be herself,' I say.

Janey flushes a little, holds my gaze and says, 'So do I.'

CHAPTER NINE

Three: A Crowd?

Wednesday, 21 March
7.35 p.m.

Dear Kitten,

Holy pole dance, there's been more dirt this evening than you'd find on a fresh turnip. Right now, I'm in the ladies at a posh Italian restaurant, taking a quick 'Kitten break' to fill you in. I've got to head back to our table, so I'll cut straight to the chase. Half an hour ago, I turn up in my cobalt-blue dress with the Marilyn Monroe halterneck and a flary skirt. Lovely. Sadly, it doesn't go with my tiger-print stilettos, so I'm in the black peep toes, which match the whole look.

Of course, when I'm shown to the table I find that mine is a spare seat at a table for three, no less. Oh, Kitten, my heart sank to see a beautiful woman with gold-blonde hair and big, dark eyes, flirting with Guy. They're giggling together before they even notice me, and she has the most delicious bare shoulders, and the most elegant neck, and, with her hair held in place in a perfect chignon, she's like a blonde version of *Pretty Woman* – at the end of the movie, mind, *not* the beginning. Anyway, eventually, Guy notices me, so he gets up, kisses me on the lips, slides an arm around my shoulders and says, 'Deborah, this is Valerie. She's my PA.'

PA? Kitten, 'confused' is not the word.

'I'm so pleased to meet you,' says Valerie, as I shake her hand. I have to admit, Kitten, she has the most delightful cleavage, and it's hard to keep my eyes away from those gorgeous, shapely breasts.

'Guy's told me so much about you,' she says, in a husky voice. Her accent, I notice, is French. I have to admit, it's sexy as heck.

'Nice as it is to meet you,' I tell her, hopefully without sounding too sarcastic, 'Guy didn't say you were coming.' At this, I eyeball Guy, who's grinning like the cat that got the cream.

'Sweetheart,' he says, in a way that makes me want to sock him, 'I thought you might enjoy it if Valerie joined us, seeing as you like the number three.'

He raises one eyebrow in a way that I don't quite understand. Then suddenly I remember him asking me about threesomes and my mouth falls open – I must look like a sodding goldfish – and I don't know whether to slap Guy or leap into this gorgeous woman's lap.

'Well,' I say, at last. 'How *lovely*.'

Guy pulls out my chair for me, like a right old gent (the toad).

Valerie bats her lashes and asks Guy, in her perfect French accent, 'Are you sure this is appropriate? Perhaps I should leave you and your lady in peace?'

Strangely enough, Guy and I both shout 'No!' at the same time. Clearly, Kitten, my reactions are complex.

So she stays. And soon I'm glad of it. Because our table is small enough that she can touch my shoulder easily, and every time she does so, little tremors of pleasure rush through me and gather between my legs. Sometimes, when we both tease Guy, we lean towards one another and Valerie whispers at my ear, her accent so smooth, her breath so warm, her scent so Chanel. And when she gets up to go to the loo, I get a lovely glimpse of her body: two perfect buttocks in that tight black dress, not to mention her long, tanned legs and lickable neckline … and that's not to mention the impeccable stilettos, which are black and spiky-heeled, and accentuate her delectable walk. In fact I watch the slit in the back of her skirt as she walks away, struck by those slender thighs, which I know would look perfect wrapped around me.

Suddenly I can feel Guy watching me, so I return to my dinner. I attempt to twiddle spaghetti round my fork, and I have to admit, there's some slurping going on, but as I dab my mouth with my napkin, I finally give in and look into his eyes. 'What?' I say.

'You're into her, aren't you?'

'She's gorgeous,' I say.

'She's my gift to you, Deborah.'

I feel a twinge of anger. 'She's not a box of chocolates, Guy. She's a woman. And so am I. You can't just toss us in the same gift bag and hope we'll suffice.'

A look of confusion furrows his forehead. 'Debs, if you don't want a threesome, you only have to say.'

It's one heck of a moment, Kitten, because suddenly I realise I actually have a choice. I can say no to this. And dammit, I don't want to! Me, slutty Debs, who's far too involved in the landlord–tenant relationship, actually wants her pussy sucked by a gorgeous French angel. All I can think of, in fact, is licking those beautiful stiletto heels, before moving on to her breasts – all tan and tight and perfect. In fact, in my fantasies I suddenly have a cock, and I'm lunging into her, Kitten, over and over, as I clamp her high-heeled shoe in my hand. Oh, God, the little French noises she'd make! And if Guy insisted on watching, that'd be fine, but I'm not sure I need him. I'd quite like to be alone with her, given the choice. What does this mean? I'm a great big poof? A fairy? A dyke? I'm all the things my mother used to say a woman shouldn't be if she wanted to avoid going straight to hell. I'm not meant to believe in hell any more, but somehow I still do. If my mother had been alive when I threw Henry out, she'd have forced me to take him back. She'd say, 'Pull yourself together, Deborah. He's a man. He's weak. Deal with it.'

But Janey says that being true to your sexual self is important. And I want to believe that. I really do.

11.50 p.m.

Dear Kitten,

You'll have to excuse my writing! I'm a scrawler when I'm tipsy. Right now, I'm in Guy's kitchen after the most sensationally unexpected sexual experience. It's amazing how a few glasses of red wine can remove your inhibitions. And my goodness, it was worth it! In fact, I'm going to write that again in capital letters so that, when I wake up tomorrow morning, I won't listen to the nagging part of me that says, 'You should have gone home last night!'

OH, MY GOODNESS, IT WAS WORTH IT!

After all, I screwed a woman tonight in all sorts of wonderful ways!

But let me start at the beginning.

So. We'd had a wonderful evening discussing all sorts of naughty things, from the most horrifying customers at Pussyfoot to Guy's confrontations with clients who try not to pay. I have to say, Guy is rather funny. He once took a swing at a man who claimed his services weren't worth the money, and, when the man in question ducked the punch, Guy went careening towards his own desk, where he ended up face-down in his own paperwork. Valerie and I were laughing all the way through … in fact, she had sidled over to me and was resting her fingers on my arm. I could feel my insides flutter at her touch, especially when she leaned towards me, and I got a proper glimpse of that magnificent cleavage! What is it about her breasts that makes me so crazy? Their tanned smoothness? Their shapely curve? The way she clearly wasn't wearing a bra? Or her nipples, which were visible through the black Lycra, their tips rising a little, like the soft nose of a cartoon dog?

Well, at last Guy gets the bill, and then we're wandering out into the darkness, with Guy's arm around both our waists. I'm a little antsy – that's Guy's word … pure American – because I want to be touching Valerie and he's made sure to walk between us. But once we're in the taxi Valerie and I are thrust together because she sits in the middle, and we start playing a game in which we girls complain about him, our lips to one another's ears, our breathing soft and hot. When Valerie whispers, 'Do we have to invite him in, *cherie*? How about *un ménage à deux*?' she lets her fingers tips brush down my front, so they gloss my own breast through the slinky material; and when I reply, my lips on her ear now, I let my fingers creep beneath her hemline where her legs are bare and smooth. 'Shall we get rid of him?' I joke, and Valerie laughs, winks, then pulls my hand up her thigh so my fingertips gloss the lacy trim of her underwear.

Oh, my God, Kitten! The purr of the car's engine drills right into me and with Valerie's hand creeping round my waist, her fingers grazing the base of my spine, I'm so turned on that I could come right there! But Guy pulls Valerie towards him, saying, 'I need to shut my secretary up!' before opening his mouth on hers and delivering a long, sultry snog. And I'm so taken by the wet slowness of their mouths that I'm not even slightly jealous. When they come up for air, they hatch a plan I can't hear, and Valerie ends up lying with her head in my lap and her heeled shoes in Guy's. He plays with her spiky stilettos, letting out soft little moans of pleasure, while I grope Valerie's gorgeous breasts through the slender layer of Lycra. Her nipples harden when I cup them and I'm utterly enchanted. In fact, feeling the warm swell of these beautiful breasts makes me long to tear off her dress and rub my tongue all over them.

Oh, my God, Kitten! How will I *ever* read this when I'm sober?

Finally, we reach the long, tree-lined avenue, full of grand houses, including Guy's. I don't even glance at the cab driver's face as Guy pays the fare. We tumble into his home, laughing together, and when Valerie takes my hand and leads me upstairs with Guy in our wake, I realise (slowcoach that I am) that she and Guy have slept together before. Suddenly, my mind's spinning with the thought of them together at work … and as it begins to dawn on me that they might fool around at his office, I tell myself, 'Don't spoil this, Debs, with a load of suspicion! You're just reacting to your past. Not every man has sex on the sly like Henry did!'

Upstairs, Guy sits on the edge of the bed and orders us around. Mr Dom himself. Fortunately, I'm all too willing to play, especially when it involves undressing Valerie, breathing in her dry perfume, peeling off that slinky dress and watching everything it slowly reveals: her lengthy legs in their spiky stilettos – so tan and slender … the black, lace-trimmed knickers that cling to her … and finally the lovely breasts with their wine-coloured nipples – a little bigger than my own, and oh, so erect! I've never been up close to a woman's breasts before, and once I throw her dress to the floor I automatically reach out to cup them. But Guy orders, 'Not yet,' and I turn to him suddenly, seeing his bare cock in his hand and his turned-on glare as he fixates on Valerie's body – I'd almost forgotten he was there.

Next, he tells Valerie, 'Undress Deborah,' and she does so, gently, her fingertips glossing my skin, sending delightful shivers through me. I can feel my pussy growing wetter at every turn, especially when Valerie's lovely eyes widen as she drinks in my legs, my pussy, my naked chest. 'I want to suck on her breasts,' Valerie tells Guy, and I want her to tell me, not Guy, and I resent him a little – until he tells her yes, that is. Because her tongue flicking against my nipples is the dirtiest thing I've ever seen. And if you think that's dirty, Kitten, wait for the part where she sinks to her knees, slides down my knickers and begins to lap at my pussy in a way I've never seen or felt before. Oh, my God, Kitten, she works me with a perfect pressure, sliding her tongue into just the right spots as I moan and gasp and bite my lip, my eyes closing, my head falling back, as the glorious heat fills me. And somehow Guy's mumblings are the only irksome thing. I mean, frankly, Guy moaning, 'All over your fucking shoes ...' is getting a little old, Kitten.

Soon he's got us on the bed, writhing all over one another, kissing each other fiercely, biting one another's lips, and when he hands us a bottle of lubricant and tells me to rub it over my tits, I don't feel like obeying him. But I do like the idea! So instead I rub the lubricant all over Valerie's tits, and I'm so aroused that my pussy starts dripping onto the sheets – oh, Kitten, who'd have guessed that a pair of tanned and slippery breasts could make me so besotted, so horny, so out of control ... those dark little nipples, those sweet swells of flesh – I swear, I could have fucked them, rubbed my clit all over them (That is what people call it, right, Kitten? 'Clit' short for 'clitoris'?). But Guy, who's kneeling next to us in nothing but his open-necked shirt, is jerking off like nobody's business. He has somehow managed to shed his trousers and socks, and there's a bright excitement in his gaze, which flits from our shoes to our breasts to our faces, over and over. His expression reminds me of a cartoon villain, all evil delight.

But I'm not really interested in Guy. I'm all about this beautiful creature with the pussy that tastes like dry champagne and the breasts that rub against mine, all slick and smooth. I'm interested in making her do the things I tell her to. I'm interested in her hair, which falls around her shoulders, trailing against her tanned skin like sunlight on sand. I'm interested in her smell – the perfumed heat that rises from her and the muskiness of her pussy. I'm interested in her words as she purrs, 'Oh, Deborah! *Mon dieu!*' and '*Oui, oui, oui!*' and the way her fingers clasp at fistfuls of my hair as I lick and suck her spiky heels, hearing Guy groaning above me. I want to hold her down and fuck her heels, Kitten! Or hump her any way I can! For the first time in my life, I want to be the boss! And I want to see her eyes filling with desire, over and over, as I have my way.

In fact, I'm all for forgetting about Guy, but he won't let me. When he orders Valerie to get what he calls 'the cock' out of a drawer, I half expect some plastic cockerel ... I'm that messed up by Guy, right now. But when she pulls out something black and glistening and ties it around her waist, I notice that it really is a penis – a plastic strap-on penis that protrudes from her trimmed pussy and makes me instantly twice as horny as I was.

And you'll never guess what happens then! I become a dominatrix! No, really. I tell her exactly what I want. I make her sit on the edge of the bed while I ride her in ecstasy, and I'm so slick that I might as well be riding a stripper's pole. I make her fuck me in the missionary position, keeping to my rhythm, and when she disobeys and goes too slow, I reach around and slap her tiny buttocks. Oh, it's sublime, and her eyes brighten! But as soon as she's worked up the perfect rhythm, I raise my arms so her beautiful breasts fall into my hands over and over again. But the hottest thing by far is when Guy asks me to stand on the floor, showing off my shoes like a supermodel, while he and Valerie kneel beside me, begging for me to place a foot in their laps, dig a stiletto heel into their thighs or push it between their lips. And I do all these things, one by one, sometimes doing what they say, sometimes doing the opposite. I'm lightheaded from these feelings of power! But the hottest thing is when Valerie plays with her toy cock while I force her to suck on my shoes. She takes the heel into her mouth, then lets me scrape it down her front so it leaves a pink line. She also lets me press her nipples with the sole of my shoe, before placing my foot on her chest and using it to slam her down onto her back. With her eyes wide with shock and arousal, she lets out three tiny 'oh's as I press her lovely black toy, which is still wet from my juices, right into her stomach.

And that's when Guy, who's standing next to us apparently, lets out a huge groan and shouts, 'You horny bitches,' and comes all over my shoe and Valerie's toy, before turning his aim and coming all over her tits as well. I'm so turned on, Kitten, that I step forward, my feet either side of Valerie's body, and use the sole of my right foot to smear Guy's come all over Valerie's breast; and that's when I feel him behind me, his breath on my ear, his fingers in me, and he fucks me – with two or three thrusts – before I feel the surge, and I come and come, over and over, staring fixedly at the substance on my shoes and the way it glistens on Valerie's nipples. I come so fiercely that I fall back into Guy, and when he catches me, and my spasms are finally over, I notice that Valerie's fingers are in her pussy and her face is heavy with the kind of bliss that forces your gaze upwards and makes you smile like a lunatic. In fact, Kitten, watching her come, bucking her hips onto her fingers, her black toy thrusting against the air, is one of the hottest moments of the night.

Thursday, 22 March

Oh, my God, Kitten, I'm a wreck.

I have to go home before they wake up. All of us slept

103

in Guy's bed last night, and when I opened my eyes I saw Guy curled around Valerie, holding her hand.

Yes, holding her hand.

He's *never* held my hand and we're meant to be dating. It was such an affectionate gesture … as if they'd been dating for years and I wasn't even in the room. He was smiling so blissfully and she looked so peaceful, curled together like embryos, or honeymooners, or dormice. Their legs were even twined together beneath the sheet that was over them. They were a mix of one another – a happy, affectionate blend.

I feel useless, Kitten. Left out and abused. And I have a hangover. And I feel like a slut. Fortunately, I have the day off, so I'm going home to lick my wounds. One thing's for sure: if I happen to walk in on Janey and Lil screwing again, I'll throw them out and bury the key.

CHAPTER TEN

Frisson at Buttercup's

Thursday, 22 March

Dear Kitten,

Well, when I got home, I was still rattled – not only by seeing Guy and Valerie curled up together, but also by my embarrassing behaviour last night. I know I vowed to be sexual, Kitten, to stop living a life that was riddled with repression, but if being sexually adventurous results in as much betrayal as being shy and unadventurous, then why should I bother?

Anyhoo, I left without waking Guy and Valerie, and got the bus home. Then once I was at my house, I couldn't find my key. So I ended up sitting on my own doorstep, emptying my bag, object by object, trying to stay calm. A few minutes after I'd started this process, the front door opened and Janey appeared. 'What you doing?' she asked, blinking, surprised.

I'd spent all this time emptying my bag, chiding myself, when I could have just knocked. 'I thought you'd be at your lectures,' I said.

'Dissertation day,' she said, gazing at the step where the innards of my handbag lay displayed: a pack of hankies, some nail polish, my asthma inhaler, my purse, a book of stamps ...

I opened my mouth to say, 'I lost my key,' but I couldn't say the words without bursting into tears.

Before I know it, Janey's clearing a space on the step by my side, sitting down next to me and wrapping an arm around me. 'Oh, Debs, please don't cry!' she says. 'Whatever happened, we'll sort it out.' And I look up through my tears, because the way she said 'we' makes me feel like I matter. 'Look,' she says, opening my pack of tissues and passing one to me, 'I was just popping out to get a pastry and some coffee from Buttercup's. Dissertation food.' She gave me a wink. 'Join me? I'll pay. I need some time off.'

And I'm so touched that I agree.

Buttercup's is a bakery round the corner from where I – or we, rather – live. I don't go in there often because it isn't en route to the bus, but once we're seated in the tiny front room, with sunlight falling warmly on our red gingham tablecloth, I feel better – especially when the rosy-cheeked waitress brings us each an almond croissant and coffee in mugs. There's a small fake carnation in the middle of the table, in a small glass vase. Not classy, but sweet. Perhaps that's a little like me.

As I tell Janey about my night, including my becoming a total dominatrix, she doesn't laugh or look amazed. She tips her head, watching me intently, her eyes so blue that it's as if they're lit from behind. Of course, I gloss over the sex, just explaining that it was way out there for me, and at times I speak in whispers because there are others nearby – there's an elderly couple next to us, each doing a crossword puzzle in a different newspaper, and behind them is a girl with a pierced nose listening to music on her earbuds … but I swear she keeps glancing across, as if she can hear me anyway.

When I get to the part about waking up to find Guy and Valerie curled together, Janey's eyes narrow with fury. The way she tears at a bit of croissant reminds me of the way Henry used to rip up junk mail. He hated junk mail, did Henry.

'This is the trouble with threesomes,' says Janey. 'People get hurt.'

I sigh. 'I should have guessed it would be a car crash,' I say.

Janey reaches across and takes my hand. 'Sweetheart,' she tells me, 'this isn't your fault. I've heard that three-somes can be wonderful. But you need strong boundaries – and everyone needs to be clear.' She says that Guy shouldn't have set up a threesome with two women he was close to. 'He could have bought a sex worker,' Janey explains, 'or asked a friend who is clearly just a mate.'

'Instead, he asked French Glamour Girl,' I say.

'He asked his PA,' says Janey. 'His PA; who he's obviously fucked before.'

'Obviously still fucking,' I sigh.

'Well, we don't know,' says Janey. 'And that's the prob.' She adds that she and Lil recently argued about a similar situation. But when she starts giving the detail, she suddenly flushes and bites her lip. 'I shouldn't,' she mutters. 'Sorry.'

Suddenly, I feel angry for no good reason. 'You can't just leave me dangling!' I snap. Janey glares at me, about to launch her defence, but I'm to blame, and I know it. I bury my head in my hands. 'I'm an idiot, Janey. I'm sorry. You're so sweet bringing me out and listening to me rant.'

In response, Janey leans forward and whispers, 'Lil's jealous of you, Debs.'

'I'm sorry?' I look right into her serious eyes. 'Jealous of *me*?'

'Well, you needn't look so surprised. You must have noticed ... our frisson.'

'Your frisson with Lil.'

Janey rolls her eyes.

'Oh,' I say, as it dawns on me. 'Your frisson with ... me.'

Janey looks adorable, all flushed and serious. There's a crumb of croissant clinging to her bottom lip and I long to reach across and smooth it away with my thumb. 'She's being silly,' I murmur. 'It's obvious you're crazy about Lil.'

'I *like* Lil,' says Janey, 'I like her a lot. But I don't lie.'

'What do you mean?' I ask.

Janey holds my gaze. 'When she asked if I had the hots for you, I told her I did.' I gawp at her, speechless. 'Problem was,' she adds, 'Lil assumed this meant I'd had sex with you. She's one for assumptions is Lil. Doesn't get it that I'm a truth-teller.'

'You are,' I say. 'I love that about you.'

She smiles. 'I know.'

I feel a warmth in my chest and a burning in my sex. 'I'm too old for you,' I tell her, amazed at my guts.

'*I'm* too young for *you*,' she tells me. Then she gives a sigh. 'Sometimes, I think I'm older than I should be. That's what comes of losing your parents so young.' My heart seems to slowly sink as she tells me how she lost her parents: her mother died of a heart attack in her late forties – so young! – and her father died of cancer only a couple of years ago.

'Oh, Janey,' I tell her, softly. 'I'm so sorry. What a strong and beautiful person you are.'

'So you see why I don't always get along with young people?' says Janey.

'Of course.' And to be honest, I almost cry when I say so, because I understand why she came across as so prickly at first. Poor, dear Janey. What a lot of pain. She's more mature than I'll ever be, Kitten. She carries it all so well.

'So I'm an old soul,' she says, with a flirty little grin. 'And, by strange coincidence, I *love* to be dommed.'

Oh. My. God. Could any response be hotter?

We watch each other, and as we do, I feel something against my shoe. Janey has somehow slid off her shoe and is stroking my foot with her own. Her gaze grows more ferocious now, as she presses her sole onto the bridge of my foot. 'The way I feel about you,' she says, 'I'm not sure I care anymore.'

What she's doing is making me tearful and wet, all at the same time. I'm just as horny as I was last night, but there's something else behind it. When Janey touches me, she touches *me* – not just the bits and pieces of me. And *this* is just footsie! But I'm not unfaithful, so I pull my foot away. 'You're with Lil,' I say, 'and until you're not, you need to stay faithful to her.'

She mutters that she's sorry and lowers her gaze. 'But I won't be with Lil for much longer.'

This fact makes me far more excited than it should, so I change the topic, saying, 'Besides, playing footsie with your boss kind of complicates things.'

She grins so warmly that I long to kiss her, and for a moment I imagine her in the outfit she'll wear if she gets a permanent job at Pussyfoot Shoes – a pleated skirt and tight pink blouse. I picture her, standing at the till, while I creep up behind her and slide a hand up her skirt. I'd feel the jolt of her body, Kitten, before she wilted with pleasure, perhaps falling over the counter, her breasts against the surface. While I explored her bottom, and she'd purr and tell me she'd been a naughty girl. That's when I'd raise my hand and …

Oh, my God, Kitten! She's my Saturday girl, for heaven's sake! Who am I kidding. This is never going to work. I'll have let her go by noon on Saturday, mark my words.

Taking a sip of my coffee, I say, 'Now, tell me about stilettos. Anything you like.'

So she does just that.

9 p.m.

I just got home from dinner with Gladys, who has the biggest mouth of anyone I've ever met. Not only because she can't stop talking about oral sex, but also because she announces my secrets *at the hairdresser's*, no less. This afternoon, there we were, in chairs next to each other, me with my usual girl, Natalie, Gladys with her gay Boy Wonder whose name I always forget, and Gladys is telling him all about her Italian boyfriend's penis. Boy Wonder and my girl, Natalie, are giggling away, and I'm rolling my eyes because really, there's a time and a place. That's when Gladys asks me, 'Why so sarky, Lady Muck? Is sucking cock too boring for a lesbian foot-fetish junkie?'

Boy Wonder and Natalie snort with laughter, but I'm so embarrassed that my mouth falls open. 'Glads! Language, please! This is my private life you're talking about!'

Gladys giggles, then turns to me. 'I'm sorry, darling. You're just too tempting sometimes.'

Still, she makes it up to me afterwards when we go shopping and she buys me a lovely new lipstick because I've told her that all is not golden with Guy. Then later, after she's bought three skirts and a red-beaded choker, she takes me to Pizza Express where she buys us a bottle of Chianti to go with our dough balls. Once they've cleared the starters, she leans across the table and takes my hand in both of hers. 'Enough of the small talk,' she tells me. 'The scoop on Guy.'

'If you joke about it ...' I warn her, hardly able to look in her eyes.

'I won't,' she says. 'I promise. C'mon.'

And if you can't trust your best friend, where's the point in trusting at all? So as soon as I've started telling her about the threesome and how we slept together, and how much I enjoyed topping Valerie, and how I woke up to find them holding one another, my eyes get so damp that Gladys has to give me a hankie. She squeezes my hand a little tighter, and leans across the table so I can smell the hairspray on her new, wavy style. And with eyes filled with kindness she says, 'It's not to do with him, love. He isn't the reason you're hurt. If you think about it, you hardly know Guy. And as for Valerie, you only just met.' Instead, she tells me, I'm mourning Henry, and seeing this clinch between Guy and his PA as a Henry-like betrayal. 'It's classic psychodynamics,' she tells me. 'Projection of painful past relationships.'

'It's shit is what it is,' I moan. 'With or without the psychobabble.'

'What's happening with Janey?' she says.

The mere mention of the girl brings me back to her presence – her serious eyes, the way she played footsie with me, the words she said about wanting me … and leaving Lil. And I look up at Gladys, in her light-pink blouse, teamed with a pale-pink crystal on a chain around her throat, and I watch her laughter lines, which I know were once pain lines. So I tell her about me sitting on the step, locked out, and Janey rescuing me. I even tell her about our game of footsie, and how I want Janey so badly, but it can't ever be.

'Not this again,' said Gladys, but her voice is gentle. 'Can't you see how exciting this is? Janey likes you too! And if she's splitting up with her girlfriend, you can give things a shot.'

But I tell her that I can't give things a shot. Janey's so young and I'm so old … But Gladys interrupts me. 'You once told me that Pussyfoot Shoes was for women of all ages. In fact you said you'd had drag queens come in – all types of women, you said.' I nod, wondering where on earth this is going. 'That's what makes the shop so enjoyable,' she says, 'that richness and variety, that sense of identity and freedom.'

'So?' I say.

Gladys shakes her head, but she's smiling like I'm adorably silly. 'Sweetheart,' she says, 'had you ever considered that your differences from Janey would make your relationship exciting?'

I look at her blankly. I'd never thought of it that way. 'But some day,' I say, 'I'll be old and past it, and she won't want me. That's how it goes.'

Gladys takes the bottle of wine and pours me another glass. 'It was *Henry* who wanted a younger woman. It was *Henry* who betrayed you. It isn't fair to assume that Janey's the same way.'

I open my mouth to tell her I'd *never* assume that. But then I notice a pain in the centre of my chest – a pain that tells me she's said something true. So I don't say a thing, just sip my wine.

'Think about it,' says Gladys.

And that's when our pizzas arrive.

11 p.m.

We have a lovely meal, and I arrived home two hours

ago. No sign of Janey, so I took advantage of the bath, using soapsuds to ease my tired feet. It's funny how store work seems to make my feet ache regardless of whether I've been working that day! I'm careful, of course, not to damage my new haircut – shoulder-length with lovely layers that move when I do. It makes me feel like a 60s girl. Janey's big book on high-heeled shoes is on the floor next to the tub, so, keeping it safe from the water, I start reading. It's fascinating stuff. Hear this, Kitten: while we were in the Buttercup Cafe, Janey told me that Catherine de Medici was the first woman to wear high-heeled shoes as a fashion accessory, because she was short – and in those days 'short' wasn't pretty for a woman. But in the *Shoe* book, it *also* says that she was marrying some powerful duke at the time and didn't feel she'd get the right respect because of her height. And that's interesting, Kitten, because we get a lot of shorter women in Pussyfoot Shoes, looking for heels that'll make them feel more powerful. And I know Gladys has apologised for mocking my interest in shoes, but still, if a shoe can give you power and confidence – and in my case, transform me into a dominatrix – that isn't a shallow affair! I mean, would Winston Churchill have taken Britain to war if he'd had less confidence? Would Princess Diana have given to all those charities if she felt all squat and unimportant?

Anyway, after half an hour or so, I hear Janey get home and turn on her music, so I climb out of the bath and wrap myself in my towel just in case she's free to say hi. It so happens she's more than free. As I walk out of the bathroom she walks out of the bedroom and we almost slam head-first straight into one another. 'Woah!' she says, lurching backwards and holding up her palms.

'Oops,' I say, and I notice her gaze running over my damp body, my cleavage, my thighs, culminating at my freshly painted toes. 'Gorgeous varnish,' she says. 'You're so pretty in pink.' Then, looking back up, she seems to remember herself. 'How are you?' she asks.

'Just had dinner with a friend.'

'*Not* Guy,' she says, and her expression surprises me. As far as looks go, it's a cross between a smoulder and a glare.

'No,' I tell her. 'Definitely not Guy.'

'Good,' she says. 'Did you see the delivery downstairs? It came this afternoon. From the arsehole himself, I imagine.'

'Oh.' I feel a little lift in my chest, but it only lasts for a second before I'm feeling sick again.

'Maybe he's feeling bad about the way he treated you.'

'It wasn't really his fault,' I say.

Janey looks me right in the eye. 'It was *totally* his fault. Insensitive bastard. If I see him again, I'll introduce him to my fist.'

Oh, my God, she's beautiful right now! So wild and dark and do-as-I-say. She's wearing a black ribby top

116

that clings to her body, and the shapes of her nipples are clear. Round her neck is a silver chain sporting a Ban the Bomb symbol. I want to grab hold of it and pull her towards me, yanking at her neck, pulling her off her guard. I want to kiss her – oh, Kitten! – all I can think of is kissing her.

She reaches out and touches my hair. 'You've had it cut. It's lovely.'

'Really?' I say.

'Gorgeous,' she says. 'And you smell lovely too,' she tells me, running a cool fingertip down my arm – it feels like she's a cool drop of water on a humid day – and the slowness of her movements ... oh, dear God, it's enough to make me jump on her, rip open her tank top and attack her beautiful body, planting my mouth on hers. 'You're fresh from the bath,' she says. And when I'm too stunned to comment, she adds, 'You're warm.' Her voice is a murmur. 'Perfectly warm.' As soon as her fingertip pauses around my elbow, she reverses her course and strokes it back towards my shoulder. I may be imagining things, but as she passes my cleavage, I swear I hear her give a sudden breath.

'Are you seeing Lil tonight?' I ask, hoping she's split up with the girl.

At this, Janey pulls back and hugs herself. 'Tomorrow,' she says. 'I have to work tonight.' And before I know it, she's giving a little wave and entering her bedroom.

Downstairs, Kitten, is a bouquet of birds of paradise, my favourite flowers in the whole, wide world. They're utterly gorgeous! I pull off the message tag, my insides light with pleasure. Maybe Janey's right about Guy feeling bad about last night.

Drum roll, Kitten. Are you ready for the big suspense? The card says, 'For my Beautiful Debs. Why? Because.' It's signed *Henry*.

CHAPTER ELEVEN

To Be or Not

Friday, 23 March

Dear Kitten,

My goodness, I was in a resplendent mood this morning!

First, we chatted about Janey's new job at Pussyfoot Shoes while we were making breakfast. I can hardly believe that she starts tomorrow! Anyway, after I filled her in a bit, we fell into talking about shoes. According to Janey, high heels restrict women's movements in order to force them to move in a different, sexier, curvier way. 'My dissertation tutor says that makes high heels sexist,' says Janey, 'but that isn't the only way of seeing it.' After all, when you restrict someone and they overcome the challenge, they grow stronger than ever. 'It's like gymnasts,' says Janey, 'when they do amazing things on the beam. The beam's a restriction, but it's one they choose to conquer, and they become more powerful when they do.' Janey also says there's a lot of sexist guff out there. After all, in the 1500s, high heels were in fashion for men as well as women. I tell her that there was a rumour a few years back that high-heeled shoes were coming in for men, but it never took on.

Janey looks angry at this, buzzing the blender for longer than usual. By the time she says, 'Typical men!' she's all red-cheeked and adorable.

'We have a drag queen who shops at the store,' I say, 'and he's a man ... you know ... technically. He comes once a month or so to buy high heels.' Then I get all confused about genders, and add, 'Does that make him a "he" or a "she"?'

Janey shrugs. 'Maybe it depends if he identifies as a woman at the time.'

'Identifies?' I ask, puzzled.

'It's a way of saying "how someone feels".'

'I suppose you're right,' I say. Then I mull for a minute. 'He doesn't *look* like a woman. Not when he's buying his shoes.' Then I pause and add, 'But should I call him a "she"?'

Janey gives me a smile. 'We'd have to ask her and see what she wants to be, right?'

These words stay with me as I stare at the birds of paradise I've placed in a vase on the windowsill. Henry never asked me who I wanted to be. He didn't even ask me who I *was*. So why, when I think of that card he wrote, and the flowers he delivered, do I feel brightly triumphant?

Janey must have caught me gazing at the flowers because she interrupted me. 'You like birds of paradise, don't you?'

'They're my favourites,' I said.

'He cheated on you,' she said softly. 'He broke the rules.' She then padded across to me, her strange, green smoothie in the glass she was holding. And before heading off upstairs, she looked me deep in the eyes and said, 'You deserve to be bought birds of paradise because your lover loves you. Not because they cheated on you and want to get you back.'

I blink at her. She looks adorable in little grey shorts and a black-and-white striped top that clings to her breasts and body. Her pale legs go on and on. She smells of cucumbers ... but maybe that's the smoothie.

'Is that why he bought me the flowers?' I ask, at last. 'Because he wants me back?'

Janey closes her eyes, gives a deep sigh, and turns away. As she leaves the room, she tells me, 'Enjoy them while you can.'

And she's right. After all, they die quickly.

Around eleven, after I've tried to sell shoes to lots of shoe-phobic customers, I get a text from Guy. It says: Haven't heard from you, Goddess. Got time for dinner tonight?

121

I stare at the text, remembering his body curled around Valerie's. I have no idea how to respond, so I don't. I'm distracted by a sudden fear that I've left the living-room window wide open, so I call Janey in case she's home. But it isn't Janey that answers.

'Janey's phone,' says Lil.

I ask if Janey's around, but I'm tongue-tied and embarrassed. I feel like I've somehow exposed my feelings for Janey, though I was obviously just panicking. But I somehow needed to hear Janey's voice. Plus she'd said it wasn't working out with Lil, yet here was the girl herself, comfortably answering Janey's calls! I admit, it made me feel twisted inside – angry from the inside out. And then, after I'd asked Lil to close the bloody window – which, it turns out, was closed after all – I feel useless again, and old, and crazy. So I dream of the birds of paradise and imagine Henry grovelling his apologies, his tears falling on my peep-toe shoes.

Anyhoo, around lunchtime, I pop out to grab myself a sandwich, but because of a load of building work I take a quieter route. This leads me behind a car park and past a betting shop, and for some strange reason I get the urge to look up. Above the betting shop is a smart-looking office with windows that are far swankier than the store beneath it. Letters are impeccably stencilled in gold on every window. They say: MALONE AND DAWES, CHARTERED ACCOUNTANTS.

Holy shit, Kitten! It was Guy's office!

It took me by surprise for a minute because I'd expected a posher place. Up above a betting shop isn't my idea of swish! But in any case, I decided to go on up. I'd surprise him; see if he wanted a sandwich. Maybe then we could talk face-to-face. And if not, no harm done.

So I find the side door, which says, 'Out to Lunch', but I know that probably means they're just up there eating sandwiches, so I head up the stairs and through another door, and the room I walk into is actually rather nice. Swanky wood panelling and floorboards and a sturdy oak desk at the centre of the room. There's a nice leather swivel chair and rows of wine-red leather-bound books. On the desk itself is a photo in a frame: a little girl who looks like Valerie, except she has gorgeous dimples and dark hair in plaits.

Each side of the desk is a door. One is ajar and the other is not. Now call it intuition, if you like, but I'm drawn towards the open one … can't seem to help myself. Maybe Guy is inside? Maybe I can catch him for lunch.

That's when I hear the first noise. A male voice moaning, 'Do it, do it.'

Up against the crack in the door, I stare into the office beyond.

I would tell you how it was decorated, Kitten. Neat or messy, suave or tacky. But these weren't the details I caught. Because Guy was lying prone on the desk, his tie loose, his shirt partly unbuttoned and his trousers down. And on top of him was Valerie.

Kitten, is it my curse to catch my lovers cheating on me, in the buff?

I get a sickly feeling at first to see Valerie's ecstatic face as she bounces on him. And he looks so much more into it than he does with me, and it's so frustrating that I can't look away – I'm just too wet not to watch. I mean, oh, my God, Valerie is hot. She's wearing a cream-coloured corset that has been pulled down to reveal her tanned breasts – and because of the way it pushes them up, they're particularly round and bouncy. She's also wearing flesh-coloured stockings and her curvy bum is magnificent as she rides up and down, up and down, harder and faster at every turn. She's wearing the same spiky shoes she wore on our date, and the light in her eyes is devilish. Her facial expression makes her look like a girl who's triumphantly laying into her playground enemy.

With her every thrust, Guy's stare moves from her breasts – not her shoes – to her pussy. His brow is furrowed and his mouth is snarly and he's saying, 'That's a good girl ... fuck me ... fuck me ...' over and over.

And it hurts to see them there doing it without me, as if I never existed, as if *I* was *their* third, not the other way around. But then again, I'm wearing these lacy knickers that rub, enjoyably, against my trimmed pussy, and Valerie looks so gorgeous as she rides him to ecstasy, her eyes glazing wildly, her hips moving in a crazed abandon, that I lean against the door post and slip my fingers up my skirt.

'Fuck, yes,' moans Guy.

And by the time I'm on the edge of climax, Valerie comes in a tearing explosion of squeals and thumping, and thrusting frenzy, and Guy groans at the very same time, shouting, 'Yes, oh, fuck it, yes ... '

And from the squelching noises Valerie's pussy is making, he must be slicked with her wetness, and that's when I come, the heat erupting, my own pussy filling with a tingly high that rises and quells, then rises and quells, then rises and rises and quells yet again.

Of course, I made one hell of a noise. That's why, when I finally come down, both of them are staring at me.

Valerie clambers off him, a look of horror on her face as she hides her boobs ... as if it matters now ... but Guy, who's presumably seen me climax, watches me with a hefty lust. 'Oh, you sexy bitch,' he murmurs, rising to his feet and climbing out of the trousers that imprison him.

I have no idea what to say. So I just stand there, stunned.

In a moment, he has me forced against the door frame with my skirt hitched up and the gusset of my knickers swept aside; and he's in me, Kitten, and I'm wet as hell, and he's fucking me and fucking me – where does he get the energy? – and as I'm about to come, high as a kite, I glimpse Valerie sitting on the desk, touching herself.

She has a blissed-out look on her face, as she whispers, 'Oh, fuck,' and watches me.

It's Valerie that makes me come like the clappers, with Guy groaning as he shoves himself into me, over and over. I might as well be fucking a silver pole – that's how hard and slick he is. But as Valerie's head rolls back and her breasts pop out of her corset again, my whole body is full of hers, and I'm dizzy with abandon.

Then, afterwards, I'm surprised to find that my face is wet with tears.

I dry my eyes as Guy pulls out of me. He tries to touch my face as he murmurs, 'What's wrong?' but surely he knows what's wrong, the arrogant bastard. 'You should have told me,' I say, with as much dignity as I can muster. 'You should have said that you two were having a thing, and *I* was *your* third.'

'It isn't like that,' says Guy, trying to reach for me, but I twist away, fumbling with my skirt.

'I'm going,' I announce.

Valerie stays silent.

'Deborah …' says Guy, 'I thought you knew this wasn't serious …'

'That isn't the point!' I snap. 'You were with Valerie and you never even said!'

Guy follows me as I march back through the front office, saying he's sorry if – it's the 'if' that gets me, Kitten – sorry *if* I thought we were monogamous.

Just as I'm rushing to get the hell away from this stupid place, I hear Valerie in the background: 'I told you we should have said something.'

But I'm practically running out of the door because all I need is a lover who's going to treat me like a goddess … and I thought Guy was going to do that. But no.

Mere minutes later, while I'm pacing down the road, my phone rings. When I see that it's Henry, I feel such a mixture of sickness and triumph because he's actually calling me that I don't know where to put myself. I mean, I'd love to hear him grovel, Kitten, and tell me he made a huge mistake. But at the same time, will I fall for him if I'm with him? Will he put a spell on me, like he did in the past? Anyway, on the phone I let him do most of the speaking. He's back in the area, he tells me. Would I like to meet for dinner tonight? His treat. He'd love to see me.

I was about to say no. Make *him* feel what it's like to be rejected, for once!

But what I really want, if I'm honest, is for him to grovel at my feet and tell me he made a horrible mistake. I want to feel wanted by him to make up for having been so *un*wanted. So I agree to the date.

And when I come off the phone, the first thing I think is: Janey can never know. Is that messed up or what?

CHAPTER TWELVE

Just a Bit of Totty

Friday, 23 March

Oh Kitten!

I arrive at the restaurant ten minutes late. Make 'em wait, Gladys always says, and it's Gladys I turned to today. On the phone, I told her about my nightmare of a lunch break, in which I came like the clappers and discovered what Guy is really like. But I also tell Gladys I'm going for dinner with an old friend. If I'd mentioned it was Henry, she'd have come round and tied me to a chair.

And, frankly, her instincts are pretty darn good.

Henry's already at our table in one of his usual grey suits – although his shirt is an almost electric blue, which is really quite bold for him. I know it sounds rude, but I'm thrilled to see that he's aged a little, his dirty blond hair a mixture of gold and grey. He's got new glasses too – a trendier pair that are blockier than his old ones. I wonder if she chose them for him, that delectable slapper of his. Predictably, he's doing the newspaper crossword when I arrive. As the waitress leads me over, I can see that he's almost filled the whole lot in.

I feel a moment of longing, up close, followed by a sickness rising in my belly. I'm not sure I should be doing this. My gut tells me everything is wrong.

When he sees me, Henry rises to his feet, eyebrows raised, and dashes to greet me. Once up close, I stay stiff enough to discourage a hug, and he awkwardly squeezes my arm. 'My dear, my dear,' he says. 'How wonderful to see you. Just wonderful.'

Immediately I'm reminded of his irritating tic. The man repeats almost every word he says. Dear God, it used to drive me to distraction.

'Hello, Henry,' I say, giving the sort of smile that a movie star gives the press.

He pulls out my chair for me and I can smell his familiar scents – aftershave, breath mints, the tang of his car's air freshener. A rush of memories gather me up, and I feel the strange, twisted memory of his body, and how it felt to lie in his arms, drunk on love, once upon a time. My poor insides feel raw when I think of it.

All the way to the restaurant I've been repeating affirmations: 'I am happy without him ...' and 'I deserve the best ... Henry praises my strapless wine-red number with its lovely flared skirt. It's the one Gladys says looks divine on me.

What he doesn't notice, of course, is my pair of tiger-print stilettos. I don't care if Guy bought them for me – they're mine and, frankly, I earned them. But of course Henry was never interested in shoes.

The conversation is slow at first. Small talk with the ex who cheated on you is never going to be a barrel of laughs. I thank him for the flowers and he says he's glad I like them. Originally, he was thinking of sending me lilies. 'Wasn't sure whether that would be too much,' he says. And after a pause, he adds, 'Just wasn't sure.'

Determined to make him uncomfortable, I look him in the eyes. 'Because lilies were in my wedding bouquet?'

Henry clears his throat, nodding. 'Precisely. I ... don't ... Precisely.'

I flap an idle hand. 'You needn't worry, Henry. I'm over you. Really.'

The look he gives me is haunting. It drains all his colour – pale as bone, he is, with those big, lost, welling eyes, and it's only now that I notice he's lost weight. His cheekbones are more pronounced than they used to be and his hair is a little floppier, as if he's trying to hide behind it. I also notice that he keeps having to push his glasses back up his nose.

He reaches for my hands and presses them together between his own. 'I made a huge mistake with you, Debsie.' He pauses and repeats, 'Huge.'

'You were more than mistaken,' I say. 'You were a cheat.' But saying these words doesn't make me feel better.

He nods slowly. When he speaks, his voice is soft: 'I threw away the most important person in my life – the most important, Debsie – just for a bit of totty.'

'Don't call her totty!' I find myself saying. 'She's a person, Henry. And you cheated on *her* too.' Holy shit, Kitten! If there's one thing I never expected it was me standing up for his mistress!

Henry's lips are parted in astonishment. His glasses slide down his nose a little and he doesn't even push them back up. He gawps at me for a long time. I thought it would feel good giving him a piece of my mind, and watching him pine for me. But it actually makes me a little nauseous.

The waitress brings menus, and Henry breaks the long silence by ordering a bottle of Sauvignon blanc, without even checking with me. I used to love it when he took charge in restaurants, but now I can almost hear Janey saying, *What does that bastard think you are? His pet?* The waitress asks what we want to eat and I end up choosing the scallops, partly because they're pricey and I know that Henry will insist on paying.

Kind of bitchy, aren't I, Kitten? And I begin to see that it doesn't suit me.

Anyway, Kitten, once we've ordered, I tell him I expect a full apology – in letter form, preferably – but now isn't the time to talk about the past. 'Tell me about your life,' I say. And of course, he does. He's moved estate agencies and is happily selling houses. He's single; he repeats this info several times. Plus he's taken up a new hobby. Golf. Henry on a golf course! I can just see him scratching his head staring into the distance. And yet, when he talks about it, his face lights up, and he's quipping about getting lost in the undergrowth, trying to find his ball.

Typical Henry. Only happy when he's playing like a boy.

Soon the waitress has arrived with our food, and he's tucking into his roast chicken and downing big slurps of wine. I click into a better mood because the scallops are soft as butter and caramelised on top, and it seems that I *have* missed Henry's company a little, not to mention his skills as a storyteller, because I genuinely giggle at some of the things he says. He tells one tale about getting stuck in a client's house because the door got wedged, and in his version he makes himself a cartoon character – a frantic, powerless little man with a goofy brain.

We both laugh. It's sweet, in its way, although I don't look into his eyes for too long.

But perhaps the most surprising thing is his newfound interest in *me*.

'How's it going at Pussyfoot Shoes?' he asks me.

I tell him I'm the manager now and he seems impressed.

'Does that mean you hire and fire people?'

Typical Henry. All about the power. Anyway, I say yes, then tell him about Janey, who's starting tomorrow.

'You gave your tenant a job?' he says. 'Is that wise, Debsie?'

I want to say, *Wiser than cheating on your wife*, but I know that's a bad direction. 'Trust me,' I say. 'She's a catch.'

'A catch?'

'Yes. Delightful.' I find myself flushing and fiddling with my necklace. 'She's a student.'

'Of what?'

'Of the stiletto heel.'

His eyes widen and he leans right forward. 'What on earth ...? What on earth is her degree?'

'Gender studies, I think.'

He gives a snort of dismissal and falls back in his chair. 'Studying stilettos in gender studies! I thought gender was meant to be all serious.' Then he gives a dismissive laugh – one that assumes I'll join in. And an old, disused part of me actually *wants* to please him and be coddled for it. But that's the old, dejected Deborah. Right now, the new Deborah is so pissed off that she almost rises to her feet and sweeps the crockery onto the floor. 'Listen, buster,' I say, 'I'll tell you a thing or two about the importance of stilettos.' And I launch into a diatribe about the feminist adoption of the high-heeled shoe. By the time I've added a few details about France in the Renaissance, where men wore high heels as well as women, Henry's looking mildly bemused.

'I absolutely believe you, pumpkin,' he tells me, smirking away, 'but still, you have to admit, it's hardly a subject for higher study.'

And there's that pet name of his. Pumpkin. The old Debs would have felt all coddled, all sweet and adored, like a puppy. But Janey would say, *How dare he objectify you!* And she'd be right.

'I'm not your pumpkin,' I say, spearing a chunk of asparagus. 'I'm your ex, who you betrayed, and Janey puts you to shame in more ways than I can say.'

His face goes even paler this time. 'Oh, Debs,' he says, covering his eyes with his hands. 'You're right, of course. But I can't help expressing affection for you.' Then he looks right at me and says, 'I knew I was still in love with you, but hearing you speak out like this … I want you more than ever.'

I open my mouth like a goldfish, then snap it shut again. Now, I know I *said* I wanted him to want me back, but sitting here, with his words hanging between us, all I feel is a need to run away. Fast. His gaze is on me like it used to be when we were first together and desire seeped from our pores, and I realise that I could go back to him if I wanted – return to the old Debs who laughed her opinions away and did everything to look after her man. But he isn't in love with me. Not really. I'm guessing he's just lonely. So I say, '*What* do you love, exactly, Henry? Apart from my new assertiveness, I mean.'

Watching me carefully, he puts down his fork, takes a sip of his wine, then leans towards me. 'You're always so real,' he says. 'You're always … just yourself.'

This throws me because I was so damn insecure with the man for so many years that I *wasn't* myself – I was waiting, as if 'being myself' would drop from the sky if I stood there long enough. In fact, even now, in my new life, I'm not sure I'm really being myself. Janey said that owning your sexuality helps you to be authentic, and I think she was right. But how, exactly, am I owning my sex life? Here I am having dinner with my ex because a man I hardly know just cheated on me and I wanted a grovelling apology from one of the bastards in my life. Here's what I do in my love life: I flit from one man to another, looking for … what? Prince Charming? A collection of sparkling compliments? A bouquet of flowers that only last until morning? Well, I'm done with that! No more 'What'll happen to me today?' I want a woman – a strong woman – a companion in life. Someone whose love stays as fresh as the day. And I know this 'someone' is Janey. And I know she wants me too. But I've not had the guts to tell her how I feel.

Then suddenly, as I'm sitting here filling our table with awkward silence, I wonder if I always date men because they ask me out. I'm just not used to *doing the chasing*. I suppose, when a woman is heterosexual, and she's attracted to the sort of men who boss the world around, *they* want to do the running, and it's easy to let them. When have I ever asked someone out?

Never, Kitten. Not once.

Under the table, I can feel my feet snugly encased in my peep-toe stilettos, and suddenly, something dawns on me: *If high-heeled shoes are meant to empower me, then dammit, I should let them.*

So I put down my fork, dab my mouth with the napkin and say, 'Henry, I'm sorry. It's been great to catch up. But if you're still in love with me, we have to call this a day.'

'I ... why?' he says, his eyes wide with surprise. His glasses slide down his nose and this time he pulls them off and squints at me across the table. 'I'm not asking for anything, Debs.'

'Neither am I,' I tell him, 'and that's precisely the problem.'

When he asks what I mean, I say that I don't want him anymore. And though saying this makes me feel like a bitch, I know I must stop being tossed around by every breeze. 'We're broken,' I tell him. 'And besides, I think I'm a lesbian.'

He gazes at me for at least five seconds, then he starts to laugh, falling back in his seat. He claps his hands together, as if he's about to applaud. 'Oh, Debs, you're adorable, but you're not a lesbian. You haven't even *been* with a woman. You've always been turned on by men.'

I tell him I have indeed been with a woman, and a beautiful woman, at that. I admit, it's satisfying to see the smirk sink from his face.

'*You've* been with a *woman?*' he says. 'A *woman? You?*'

'And a man,' I say, 'both at once, actually.'

Behind us, I hear somebody mutter, 'Holy Moses,' and I notice that the tables around us have gone quiet. It's strange, but I really don't care what anyone thinks, right now.

Henry glances around, then whispers, 'Debsie, you're loud.'

'I *am* loud,' I announce. 'Especially when I'm in bed with a fellow lesbian.'

'You are not a lesbian,' says Henry. 'Pumpkin, you're not, you're just confused.'

Now there's some tittering behind us and the clink of glassware.

'Oh, really?' I say, snarkily. 'Well, how come, when I caught you fucking that woman, *she* was the one I was watching, not you?'

'What?' he says. 'You were watching *Sarah?*'

'*Sarah* was gorgeous. *You* faded into the background.'

He opens his mouth, then closes it again, then opens it again and lets his jaw hang there. 'You're not into women. You can't be into women. You were always so

137

into my ...' He points down at his lap like some kind of pantomime character.

'Your cock, Henry,' I announce, as he frantically gestures for me to keep down the noise. I have to admit, the surrounding tables have turned so silent that a whisper wouldn't cut it. Janey will be proud if I tell her about this. 'Women can have cocks too,' I say. 'It isn't about what bits you have.'

He looks terrified, stunned, as he shakes his head slowly. 'You're not,' he says, more quietly now. 'Even if you don't want *me* anymore ... you can't. You're not. Not *you*.'

'For someone who says he's in love with me,' I say, 'you have a funny habit of refusing to acknowledge me.'

'Debsie, I'm sorry, but listen to me for a moment –'

'Believe what you like,' I say. 'Why should I care?'

And I still feel his eyes on me as I collect my handbag and stride from the room, with the whole world watching.

CHAPTER THIRTEEN

Give a Queen a Stiletto

Saturday, 24 March
12.30 p.m.

Dear Kitten,

Last night, after I stormed out on my date with Henry, I came straight home and did two things. The first was to bin the birds of paradise he sent me. The second was to call Glads for a friendly ear.

'Bigoted bastard,' she tells me, when I've given her the spiel.

'He's just defensive,' I tell her. 'What puzzles him most is that I always seemed into his cock!'

'Oh, the ego!' Gladys snorts. I do too.

'Mind you,' she says, once we're both done with laughing. 'A lot of men think it's all about that. And it isn't. It really isn't.' She tells me how her new man, Marco, isn't very well hung at all. Then she adds that what he does with his hands and mouth is beyond compare. 'Plus his accent!' she gushes. 'And he's so *intelligentsia* that, when he rails against Milgram's electric shock technique, I end up jumping his bones.'

I roll my eyes.

'And you,' she says, 'you're a sexually political beast! Coming out in front of all those people! You're rebellious, Debs. I didn't know you had it in you.'

I don't know how to take that last bit. I mean, of course I have it in me to rebel! All the same, when I try and think of an instance, I can't. Glads is right. This is my first rebellious move. And at the thought my lips spring into a smile.

Then, this morning, when I notice Janey isn't up, I consider waking her. But I decide I should trust her. She'll be at Pussyfoot Shoes by eight, just like she said she would. All the same, I put out her strawberries and spinach, ready for her to make her breakfast smoothie. I place the blender next to them, feeling all warm inside – I love doing things for Janey. It makes me glow.

And maybe it's rash, but I also leave her a note that says, 'Have a nice breakfast and see you at eight. P. S. I have binned the flowers.'

Now, bear with me, Kitten, because I need to explain what happened when Janey did arrive. See, head office had emailed me the usual printed directions for what a trial member of staff should wear, and I'd forwarded them to Janey. Basically, Pussyfoot Shoes stipulate: for men, a pair of black trousers with a crisp white shirt and tie, and, for women, a flared pink knee-length skirt with a plain white top.

Does Janey keep to these instructions? Well, frankly, it's hard to say. Because when she arrives at the shop, bang on the dot of 8 a.m., she's wearing a pair of black trousers, a crisp white shirt and a long silver-and-black-striped tie. A tie, Kitten! A swankier one than Henry would ever wear – more Guy's taste, I'm guessing. But, my God, the girl looks far hotter than those men ever could. On her head is a flat-peaked cap, and on her feet a pair of black pointy lace-ups. And her eyes are a defiant blue as she stands in front of me. Her head is cocked and she has one hand on her shoulder, like a character from a gender-bending musical. There's a twitch of a smile at the edge of her lips and a brightness in her eyes. 'Well,' she says, 'how do I brush up?'

'Um, wow,' I say, running a hand through my hair. I gaze at her for a moment, trying to fight my urge to grab her tie and yank her towards me, before swooping my lips to hers. The more I drink her in, the damper I feel between my legs. Oh, my God, Kitten, she's deliciously distracting! I picture her lying sideways along my double bed, naked except for her cap, her tie, and a pair of black lacy briefs. The tie is draped across her lower breast, but her other is totally naked, with its hard, rosy nipple just begging for my lips.

'Well?' she says, giving me a devilish look. She leans against the doorpost, like a guy who's coming on to me. 'Do I look dapper, or what?'

'You look incredible,' I say. I reach out and run her tie through my fingers. It's warm from the heat of her body. Half of me wants to kiss her, while the other half wants to take her over my knee and spank her, hearing her gasp with pleasure every time she feels my palm.

Christ on a crumpet, what am I thinking? I glance up and down the street to see if anyone saw us, and once I know the coast is clear I tell her to come inside. Then I explain my concerns about her get-up. For one, 'Crabby Carol' the Area Manager will be coming this afternoon, and she won't take kindly to gender-bending. Also, how will our customers react?

'Well,' says Janey, 'I could take off the tie.' She cocks a sexy eyebrow. 'But it'd be a shame, don't you think?'

'Janey, love,' I say. 'We're here to make money, not political points.'

'I did it for you,' says Janey, standing so close that I can feel her breath. (Dear God, Kitten! She smells of strawberries!) 'You threw the flowers away. So I thought I'd get all queer in celebration. After all, I finished with Lil, last night.'

Oh, joy! 'And, as of yesterday, I'm finished with Guy,' I say, beaming away.

142

'Really?' Her whole face lights up and she claps her hands like a birthday girl. 'I thought you went out on a date last night.'

'No,' I say. And I decide not to mention my dinner with Henry. What good would it do anyway?

We look at one another, smiling, for an awkwardly long time. At last I say, 'This is all wonderful. But this is business, love, OK?'

That makes Janey's look go sour. 'I'm wearing what it says in the guidelines you sent me. I mean, I was *impressed* that they didn't mention gender.'

I think for a second. But it's hard to think when the woman of your dreams is:

a) single for the first time since you both met;

b) looking so incredibly hot;

c) gazing at you with such angry passion that you wonder if she's going to jump your bones;

d) still looking so incredibly hot.

Then suddenly, I'm thinking: I'm in love and lust with a twenty-three-year-old woman; last night, I told my ex-husband and half a busy restaurant that I was a dyke; and I'm becoming a sexual radical. Is that a recipe for conventional clothing? I think not.

So I say, 'All right. We'll let it ride this morning and I'll ask you to take off the tie by noon. Then, at four, when the Area Manager turns up, you'll be safe as houses.'

Janey gives a sigh and stares down at her hands. 'OK,' she says. 'Thanks.'

And I feel like a party pooper.

But here's the funny bit. The customers *love* her!

Young women clip along in brand-new shoes and flirt with her, asking if their bum looks good, giving her moon eyes as she unpacks shoes from tissue. A smart, older woman, who's dripping in silver jewellery, says that Janey reminds her of her lesbian daughter. ('I'll be coming back here more often,' she says. 'We should see more smart women like you dressing in shirts and ties.') A girl with long red curls held back by black hair combs asks for seven pairs of shoes to try. Seven! And Janey brings them so willingly and is so absorbed in choosing which pairs suit her customer that she ends up kneeling on the floor to get a closer look. I tell her not to do this, of course. Kneeling like nuns isn't our style! But the girl buys two of the seven pairs and seems delighted with Janey.

What's more, after a mere hour and a half she understands the storeroom system as if she's been working here for years, and is using the till like a genius.

But me? I'm not at my best. I'm glancing over my shoulder at Janey every minute, noticing her perfect buttocks inside those fitted trousers as she bends over to pick up a box, or I'm watching her smile as she rings up a pair of mules, or imagining whether she's braless underneath her shirt and tie, her nipples all hard and

144

pink, her breasts a swell of pale skin. All I want to do is slam her against the wall and open my mouth on hers, running my hands across her chest and feeling her nipples hardening beneath. I want to rub my pussy against her thigh, Kitten, and run the edge of my peep-toe stiletto up and down her trousered shin, showing her how much I love her like this – all gender-bending and kinky.

Pearl arrives at eleven. She's less excited about Janey's outfit. In fact, she looks a bit peeved. 'I don't see why I can't wear something like that,' she says.

'Pearl, I had no idea you liked to wear a tie!'

Pearl flips her blonde hair behind her shoulders. 'I told you how much I hate flared skirts. I'm a pencil-skirt woman.'

I tell Pearl that Janey's outfit is temporary. Next weekend, she'll be wearing a Pussyfoot uniform.

'You've made a decision on this new girl quickly, haven't you?' She crosses her arms, gives a look that says, *Well?*

I butter her up and remind her how splendid she is, and all is forgotten.

But back to the smut, Kitten! At one point, Janey and I are both in the stockroom, and Janey is up on the stepladder, reaching for a super-small size. As I slink past her, my eyes are level with her bum and, dear God, I get so close to pawing her through the material and feeling those smooth buttocks that I almost lose my mind. Then, when she's climbing down, and I'm on my way back, shoebox in hand, she smiles, reaches out for me and pulls me into a hug. It's a surprise because we've never hugged before. 'I'm sorry I got pissy about the tie,' she whispers. 'I'm so grateful for this job, Debs. And I love wearing this get-up too.'

She brushes her hand up and down my back, super-slow, so I can feel my every cell warming with her touch, and our breasts are pressed together, and her jawline smells of that soap of hers, and her cheek is so soft as she pulls away.

'I'm ... glad you ... like it,' I stutter. 'You're ... a great fit.'

'Mmm,' she purrs, running her fingertips idly down my bare arm. Her eyelids grow heavy, and she looks up at me through her lashes. 'You and I work well together,' she murmurs, 'wouldn't you say?' I can feel my arousal all over my body, as if sexy women are blowing warm air all over me, kissing me behind my ear and down my breasts and thighs ...

Then comes the real corker! Before she pulls away, she rests her cheek against mine and says, 'I know I look all "man" today but, just so you know, I'm wearing the skimpiest pair of satin knickers under here. They're black and lace-trimmed and totally femme. They rub against me in lascivious ways.'

As she moves away, I stand there, mouth agape, my

flesh in a personal hell of longing. I want to kiss her hard, up against the boxes of shoes, letting them collapse around us as I rip off her clothes ... Oh, Kitten, I'd hump her like a crazed dog, rubbing myself against those lovely toned thighs, squeezing those perfect breasts of hers and rutting her ... yes, rutting!

Needless to say, by the time my lunch break comes around, my knickers are damp, my heart is pumping, my body feels as warm as if I've been sitting near an open grate. But Janey's in the restroom, so I can't go and touch myself, and waiting for her to come out is too much to bear. So I rush towards the café as quickly as I can, the wind blowing my umbrella inside out. On the way, I get a call from Area Manager Carol, who tells me that when she turns up she'd like a word with Pearl as well as Janey, so she'll be getting there a little early. 'Kill two birds with one stone,' she says. 'Maybe you and I can find a minute too?'

For a moment, I wonder if Pearl has complained about Janey's outfit. But no. Pearl's more loyal than that. So I tell Carol I look forward to seeing her.

So now here I am, journalling at the cafe, sipping my tomato soup. I'm still feeling an obsessive burn between my thighs, Kitten, and the lacy knickers that I'm wearing today rub against my pussy every time I squirm. I'm turned on by the rough softness of my own underwear! I feel like I'm a schoolgirl again!

2 p.m.

Dear Kitten,
Oh, dear God, where to start?

Back at the store, there's no sign of Pearl, and I find Janey serving Billie, my drag queen. Today, Billie's a woman, which isn't always the case – mind you, like Janey says, 'being' a woman isn't about your bits. Right now, Billie's a dark-skinned goddess, with broad shoulders and corkscrew curls. Her top is strapless, shimmery and silver, and her lips and fingernails are blood-red. As she strides up and down in a pair of silver high-heeled sandals, I watch her deliciously lengthy legs and the rock of her splendid buttocks. When she spots me, she patters a wave, then places a hand on the choker around her delicate throat: a string of see-through stones, bound together with metal links.

'Your new girl's a natural,' she tells me, touching my shoulder. 'And I love, love, love her outfit!'

I glance over at Janey, who gives me a cute, cocked smile before turning to tidy some shoes into boxes.

'She's gorgeous, isn't she,' I say, as Janey bends over a little, and her round bum cheeks rise up. Again, I'm thinking of pulling down her trousers and smacking that lovely round bum.

'Did you know she's studying the stiletto heel?' says Billie.

'Oh, yes,' I say. 'She's a bright spark, our Janey.'

Aware that I'm all moon-in-June, I change the topic by asking Billie if these shoes are for a drag show, but she says she's actually meeting her boyfriend's parents this evening and wants to look utterly stunning. 'You're always stunning,' I say, 'and holy hotdog, these shoes are divine on you!'

'They're crazy if they're not impressed with you,' says Janey. And soon I'm ringing up Billie's purchase as Janey packages the seven-inchers in layers of tissue with an artist's care. 'These heels are spectacular,' sighs Janey.

'Perfect for hurling at cops,' says Billie, and laughs.

Janey titters.

'Did I miss something?' I say.

Billie says that she and Janey have been talking about Stonewall. I don't know what Stonewall is. So Janey explains that the Stonewall Riots happened in the 1960s in a New York bar. 'The police were arresting everyone for being queer,' says Janey, 'but one of the queens – Sylvia Rivers – she wasn't having it. So she took off her stiletto and hurled it at a cop.'

'Bang, bang!' cries Billie, clapping her hands. 'Give a queen a stiletto and she'll make it a bomb!'

I grin. *Bang, bang*! I like that. Stilettos as a big, bad weapon! 'People who say that shoes can't be deep don't understand what they stand for,' I say.

'Perfectly said, as usual,' says Janey, as she brushes

my hand with hers, and she lingers for a moment, and I can smell her shampoo and feel the warmth coming off her, and oh, oh, oh ...! I barely even say goodbye to Billie because I'm so close to Janey, and I can feel us swaying towards each other, her lips so close, her breath so warm, her fingertips stroking up my arm and resting round my jawline. Suddenly I'm not in the real world any more, I'm just sinking towards her, and she's rising on tiptoes, and the smell of coconut soap is filling my head, and her soft lips are way too close, and I whisper, 'God, you're perfect,' and she says, 'God, you're delectable,' and I whisper, 'I hope you know you've got the job,' and she says, 'What are you doing for dinner tonight?' and I say, 'Nothing, as yet,' and she says, 'If you get hungry, maybe we could eat?' and I say, 'Oh please!'

And she leans in closer, her eyes growing heavy, and I'm dizzy with wanting her, giddy with her warmth. But the doorbell tinkles and we spring apart, and I look up to see a couple of girls in black ribby tops and light denim jeans. 'I'll take these,' says Janey, turning away, trailing her fingers along the counter.

Where the hell is Pearl? She isn't answering any of my calls. What if Carol turns up and I don't know where Pearl is? I don't want to lose another member of staff, especially Pearl, whom I love. Turns out Janey's so efficient that I'm at a loose end, so I tell her to text when she needs me, and now I'm in the back office doing some paperwork.

Outside, the rain hasn't stopped. There's even a rumble of thunder.

All right, Kitten. I warn you, this is a soap opera of an afternoon.

Fifteen minutes into my paperwork, Janey does indeed text, so off I go to help. When I arrive on the shop floor, Janey's talking to a man and her voice sounds cool. Maybe it's because he's male – does Janey have a problem with men? The man in question has his back to me but, with that slightly stooped posture and a suited torso, he looks strikingly like Henry.

As I walk across, Janey is telling him, 'I don't believe you. I *know* she would have told me.'

For a moment, my heart freezes. What's going on?

Then I hear the man say, 'Maybe, but did she tell you that we went for Italian last night?' And, dear God, that's Henry's voice! Janey is talking with Henry!

'What's going on?' I call.

Henry turns towards me. 'Hello, darling! Just wanted to see the shop for myself –'

'What have you been saying to Janey?' I snip.

Janey stares at me with a look that's a mix of horror and fear. 'You went to dinner with him?' she asks, her voice soft and faraway. 'You said you didn't have a date last night. That's what you told me.'

'It wasn't a date!' I say. 'We went out to talk.'

Janey has flushed an angry red. 'Is this before or after you dumped Guy?'

'Janey, don't let him –'

But Henry butts in: 'Who on earth is Guy?'

'Will you both listen!' I snap.

But Janey turns away, a hand in the air. 'I'm done with this,' she snaps. 'You leave one liar and you end up with another.'

'He's my ex!' I call, but it's too late. Janey tosses her name-tag over her shoulder and leaves the store, the door swinging in her wake.

When I turn back, Henry is smiling a warm smile. 'All a big misunderstanding,' he says. With that he steps towards me, as if to kiss my face, but I jerk out of his reach.

'It certainly is,' I say. 'That was not a date last night.'

'It was an Italian meal,' says Henry. 'What's *not* a date about Italian?'

'We never called it a date.'

'So? I'd sent you birds of paradise, Debsie! What did you think I wanted? To catch up?'

'To apologise!' I snap. 'To say sorry for fucking up my life! And now what are you doing? Fucking up my life. Again.'

He runs a hand through his hair. Suddenly, he has the expression of a wounded pup. 'Debsie,' he says, his shoulders slumping. 'I just ... You're having a fling with that Janey girl, aren't you?'

'Sadly, no,' I say.

'Oh?' He says, a glimmer of hope in his voice.

'But I want her,' I add. 'Who wouldn't?'

His brow furrows as he launches across the room, striding up, as if he's late for a flight. He takes me by the shoulders, and it really hurts! But when I tell him to let go, he doesn't. Instead, he leans right in, crushing me in his hands, and says, 'I know it's my fault that you've begun these crazy fantasies, but if you'll let me make it up to you, I'm ready.' He breathes on my face, his lips close to mine. 'Jesus, Debsie,' he says, 'you're a man's woman! Look at you! You're stunning. Why on earth do you think you're a lesbian?'

'Don't tell me what I am,' I snap, trying to wriggle away. 'Take your hands off of me,' I say, but his grip is like a pair of iron cuffs.

'You are the most insufferable woman,' he says, and suddenly, he's forcing his mouth on mine and kissing me, hard, like he's Humphrey Bogart and I'm a femme fatale. For a moment, I revel in it because, my God, Janey has made me so wet, the wanting of her, the way she makes me palpitate when she's in the room ... and I can feel him hardening against me, pressing into me, and I almost relax into feeling it all. But after a second, I push him away. And in the same moment, the rain outside grows heavy.

'Leave now,' I tell him.

'Didn't you feel that?' he asks me. He grabs my wrists to pull me back. And when I wrench myself away, I stumble and find myself propelled backwards. I flail my arms, losing balance on my peep-toe heels, and end up falling against a display table, my butt thumping into a host of metallic shoes.

'Get out,' I tell him, struggling back to my feet, as stilettos and ballet pumps topple around me.

'You're coming home with me,' he says, pacing towards me again. 'We're going to pull ourselves together.'

This time, I use a voice I've never had to use before. It comes right up from the depths of me, rough and hard. 'Some of us don't need to pull ourselves together!' I shout. 'Some of us just need to call the police and get our bastard husbands to leave this bloody shop!'

Just then, I realise I'm holding a silver stiletto that I must have grasped when I stumbled into the display. And seeing as he's standing there, like a stubborn fool, I lob the shoe right at him. 'This,' I shout, 'is Stonewall.'

'What?' he says, jumping out of the way.

Then I pick up another stiletto and another, and lob those at him too, so he's ducking to avoid them, and telling me to calm down. And as he waves his arms and shouts, 'Debsie, this is crazy!' I pick up a gold slingback and nearly hit the mark, getting him right on the edge of his thigh. 'Jesus!' he shouts, 'you could hurt a man with those!'

'That,' I say, 'is just the effect I was after.'

'Debsie –'

'Get out of here,' I say, picking up a strappy sandal. 'I'll give you one more chance before I call the police.'

'All right,' he says, throwing up his hands 'OK. I'm going, OK?'

As I raise a suede platform – rather a nice one, with silver-studded heels – he turns and rushes from the shop. For a moment there is silence. I gaze around at the mess, stunned by what just happened. Only now do I notice a customer in a pink cloche hat, cowering gingerly in the corner of the store, clasping a pair of court shoes to her chest, her lipsticked mouth in the shape of an 'O'.

I neaten my hair and pull myself upright. Hurling the stock around certainly isn't a super-savvy marketing ruse. 'Sorry about that,' I say. 'Now, how may I help you?'

But she's already putting the shoe down, making her excuses and running from the shop.

I sigh. What an afternoon! I feel like crying. Janey, it seems, has sent me a text: You know how I feel about you, it says. How could you date him behind my back? You and Lil can have one another. I feel so sick that I have to grab my head. I'm done with liars, Janey continues. I'll leave my rent on the kitchen table.

Within moments, I'm locking up the store and dialling for a taxi, so afraid of losing Janey that I keep forgetting to breathe …

CHAPTER FOURTEEN

Stripped Down

Saturday, 24 March

Kitten, all I know when I open the front door and rush upstairs to Janey's room is that I have to stop her. She was only a few minutes ahead of me, so she can't have packed up yet, surely ... but a part of me is panicking as if she's already gone.

I burst into her room, and come to a standstill when I see her there. She's on the other side of the bed, picking her underwear out of an untidy stack of clothes and piling it up. Little briefs, coloured black, grey and white, lie in a pile near her pillow. She doesn't look up at me. Neither does she stop folding.

'I'm sorry!' I gasp. 'Don't go!'

She freezes, sighs, places a pair of briefs on the stack. Then, at last, she meets my gaze. 'This isn't going to work, Debs.'

'It is! It can!'

She shakes her head. 'Why aren't you with him?'

'Because I don't *want him.*' I tell her how I did go to dinner with him last night, but only to hear his apology. Then, when I see her eyeing me suspiciously, I add, 'Well, to be honest, I'd just finished with Guy, and I thought I could do with some grovelling.'

'You didn't think to call me up?' I'm about to answer, but she returns to her folding, mumbling, 'No, because I'm a woman, and you're not into women.'

'But I am,' I tell her, walking up to the bed. 'I'm into you. And *you're* a woman.'

I sit there, watching her slender fingers as she expertly folds her last couple of briefs. All I want is for her to run those fingertips across my cheekbone, down my jaw, between my breasts, right down into the core of me. All I want is to feel them, superlight, against my clit, circling, circling … She moves on to T-shirts next, folding, folding. For a while we sit in silence, my heart thumping.

'Are you still here?' she says, with a glare.

'You can't leave.'

My words pull her up straight. Exasperated, she says, 'You've broken my heart. Why the hell would I trust you again?'

I rise to my feet and walk round the bed, feeling the angry heat in my chest. 'Janey, Pearl's gone walkabout and Carol the Area Manager is going to find the store locked up, with shoes strewn higgledy-piggledy all over the floor.'

Janey does look up now, filled with alarm. 'You closed the store early?' She holds her head. 'You left shoes all over the floor?'

'I was throwing them at Henry,' I said. 'He refused to leave.'

Janey's lips twitch upwards at the corner. 'You threw … shoes … at Henry?'

'Damn right I did. Like Stonewall.'

It takes a moment for Janey's face to light up. 'Ah,' she says at last, 'shoe-throwing! Brilliant!'

I glow a little then. 'Well, anyone who thinks they can treat me like that has another think coming.' Automatically, I start to straighten her tie. 'I even threatened to call the police.' Then, under my breath, I add, 'I think I may have scuffed one of the gold Guess pumps, actually. That'll have to come out of my pay. Bang goes my trip to Spain with Glads.' I smooth the tie against her front, running my fingertips over it, before neatening the collar and sweeping a hair from her shoulder.

Janey reaches out and cups my face with both her hands. And with a concern void of rage she says, 'Debs, if Pearl's gone, who's minding the shop?'

Our lips are so close I go blurry. 'No one,' I say, vacantly.

'But the Area Manager's coming!'

'I know.'

'But Debs, you might lose your job!'

'Don't you get it?' I say, clasping her shoulders. 'Given the choice, I choose you.'

She searches my gaze, then her eyes start to fill. 'That's crazy,' she says.

'I know, but –'

And suddenly, she pulls my face to hers and kisses me. Oh, my God, Kitten, it's unlike any other kiss! Longer, smoother, more passionate, more steamy. She tastes of fruity lip balm and the remnants of coffee, and her lips are so soft as they press and press, moving to touch every bit of my mouth, keeping me coated in her. Our bodies sink together, and I can feel the heat rising from her, seeping into my cool hands, making them warm. I drift into a dream-state where there's nothing but this kiss – the damp of it, the curve of it, the endless, ardent sex of it – and I press my thirsty groin onto her thigh, trying to grind against her and get the release I crave. I swear, it feels so good that I'd have humped her, right there, climaxing hard with just a few grinds – that's how wet I've become – except Janey pulls back, snapping me out. 'That was one hell of a kiss,' she whispers.

'Don't stop,' I say.

She reaches for her phone. 'Sweetie, there isn't time. We're going back to Pussyfoot.' And before I can stop her, she's ordering us a cab.

Still giddy from our cab ride, during which I wove my fingers through Janey's and felt my heart rise like a balloon, we arrive to find Crabby Carol the Area Manager talking to Pearl inside the shop. Pearl! Thank goodness! Perhaps she opened the shop again before Carol appeared. In I walk, making both the women turn. Janey is right behind me. I can smell her coconut soap, and, dear God, it's distractingly good. 'Ah, Carol,' I say, before turning to Pearl. 'Sorry, we had an emergency.' I glance towards Pearl. 'Is everything all right, Pearl, dear?'

But Pearl's face has gone paper-pale. She shrugs before staring at her hands.

Crabby Carol folds her arms. She looks particularly fierce today. Think shoulder pads, a blunt-cut bob, trendy glasses with thick black rims, perfect lipstick, manicured nails and a pair of blue-green eyes that seem unnaturally close together. She also has a small, yet beaky, nose that always makes me feel as if I'm being inspected by a starling.

'Well, look who decided to join us,' she says. As soon as she spots Janey, she gives her the once-over, before wrinkling her nose as if she's sensed a bad smell. 'Please tell me this isn't your new Saturday girl?'

'Janey?' I say. 'She is. Doesn't she look … dapper?'

Crabby Carol frowns at me, raising a single eyebrow. 'When I got here, the lights were on, the store locked and the "Closed" sign was up.' She glances at her watch. 'That was about ten minutes ago, and just as I was trying to work out what on earth was going on, Miss Gilsworth here –' Carol looks at Pearl, who seems increasingly shifty '– Miss Gilsworth came and let me in. And judging by the look on her face as she picked her way across a medley of discarded shoes, she had no idea what had been going on.'

'I was in the loo,' says Pearl. 'I had a ...' She flushes. 'A woman's emergency.'

I smell a rat. Pearl had sneaked off for a fag, and both of us know it.

'Debs had an emergency too,' says Janey.

But Carol glares at her with such violence that Janey flushes and bites her lip.

'That,' Carol tells her, pointing at her tie, 'is not suitable for Pussyfoot Shoes. Remove it at once.'

Janey glances at me before sighing and starting to undo her tie. But I have to say, I don't like Carol's tone. 'None of this is Janey's fault,' I say.

Janey nudges me really hard. 'No, it really isn't!' I tell Carol. 'I –'

'All three of you,' interrupts Carol, 'are in serious hot water. You all abandoned the store without calling head office. And I doubt all three of you had an emergency *all at the same time.*'

For a moment, there is silence. I can feel my stomach sinking like a rock. I realise that I could make up an elaborate lie, like the Emergency Room visit we concocted in the cab, although I'm sure Carol knows that ER never takes less than half an hour.

'You know what,' I tell Carol, suddenly, 'you're absolutely right. I unclip my name tag and hold it towards her. 'I've had a wonderful time working here. Really, I have. But I can't imagine you'd let me off if I told you my emergency was an affair of the heart.'

Carol takes the badge, but looks confused. 'You had a heart attack?' she says.

I can feel Janey next to me, trying not to laugh.

'I had to go and stop the woman I love from leaving,' I tell Carol, 'and if that isn't an emergency, I don't know what is.'

'*Love?*' says Carol, as if it's a foreign word. 'I'm sorry; let me make sure I've got this right. You left Pussyfoot Shoes unmanned ...'

'Un*woman*ed,' says Janey.

I try not to laugh.

Carol tells Janey that if she wants the opinion of a Saturday girl who is well and truly sacked, she'll ask for it.

'Now, wait a minute,' I say. 'You haven't heard Janey's explanation yet.'

'I'm not listening,' says Carol. 'Not to any of you. Why on earth should I trust you? You abandoned the store, showed an utter lack of judgement, and the only person who has any excuse is Pearl Gilsworth here, who, I might add, won't be getting the manager's job *in spite* of the vacancy.'

Pearl's cheeks and neck have flushed scarlet.

'That's a horrible thing to say!' I announce. The anger is burning inside of me. The woman's obviously going to sack me, but how dare she do it so callously! The least she could say is 'Thank you for your service.' And surely I deserve the word 'regrettably', at least.

'You,' says Crabby Carol, pointing right at me, 'will receive the balance of your pay. You will return your uniform and –'

'Oh, this?' I shout, reaching for my blouse. 'This old thing?' I add, as I pull my blouse right open, exploding two buttons that ping towards Carol and Pearl. 'Well, for your convenience, I'll give it to you now,' I shout, dropping my blouse on the floor, before unzipping my skirt and letting it pool around my black five-inch stilettos.

As I stand there in my white sculpted cotton bra with matching knickers and suspender belt, my fists on my hips, Janey gives a whoop. 'Oh, shit!' she cries, applauding. 'You're so fucking perfect!'

Carol stands in horrified silence, her mouth hanging open, two tiny spots of redness appearing on her cheeks.

'Come on, Janey,' I say, taking her hand. 'It's time for the big seduction, you handsome devil.'

And out we walk, hand in hand, with yours truly in nothing but her undies.

164

In the street, Janey pulls me into her arms. I can feel the giggles fluttering through her. 'That,' she says, 'was the most romantic thing that ever happened to me.'

'Are you sure?' I say, as I rest my head against hers. 'After all, I am near-naked in the middle of Chipham High Street.'

'It's *our* Stonewall,' says Janey, kissing my hair. 'Plus you're the most beautiful woman I've ever seen.'

As people walk past in their dozens, glancing at my lack of clothes in shock or bemusement, all I can feel is my warmth against Janey's.

And my, how I glow.

CHAPTER FIFTEEN

Magnificent

Saturday, 24 March

Now, Kitten, here's the thing ... when a girl offers you the shirt off her back, you know that she more than likes you. I'm naked when Janey does just this and we're rushing towards the taxi rank, trying to avoid the wolf whistles, dirty jokes and sneers. It's just as well that I'm getting so much attention, because it stops me from obsessing about the heaviness of my breasts, the puckering of my upper arms, the curve of my belly ... At one point some little bastard takes several photos – but if I will strip off in the middle of town, I suppose I can hardly complain. It's the attempt to photograph me that pushes a flushed, defiant Janey into loosening her tie and offering me her shirt. 'Don't!' I say. 'I want to undress you myself!'

'That's rich coming from you,' says Janey, with a wry grin and cocked eyebrow. 'Anyway, I want to cover you up. When the world is looking at my naked beau, am I meant to be unpossessive?'

'*Beau*?' I say, tickled by the French. 'You're *possessive*?' I add, tickled by the romance. But I manage to persuade her to keep the shirt on. 'You're causing as much fracas as I am,' I say, reminding her that gender-bending is hardly the norm in this small-minded town.

A guy across the street gives us a catcall. I mock-salute him, which makes him rock with laughter.

'Debs,' says Janey, 'gender-bending is child's play compared to public nudity.'

Fortunately, I suddenly see a taxi driving past, and though I'd usually be too late at this distance, today my nakedness makes us lucky.

'I'm actually booked,' says the driver, when we climb in, 'but naked ladies come up trumps.'

Janey snorts.

'Well?' says the driver, glancing back. 'What's the story? I deserve that much, don't I?'

I give him a potted version of the story, but Janey's placed her hand on my knee and is trailing it softly up my stockinged leg, hovering around the clip of my suspender belt and tracing tiny circles. 'You're stunning,' she whispers in my ear. 'I've never been so turned on.'

She trails her fingers back down to my knee – up and

down, up and down – so that every inch of my stockinged flesh is purring and begging for more. I grab her hand and drag her fingers slowly up beyond my stocking-top, up across the naked flesh, watching her eyelids grow heavy with lust, as her gaze flickers over me, drinking me in. Then I slide my own hand down my belly before stroking my lace-trimmed briefs and feeling my pussy through the layer of cotton. I arch, appalled at how wet I am – God, with Janey's eyes on me like this I could come any second … and part of me thinks, Fuck it, why not, which is why I take Janey's fingers and press them onto my briefs, whispering, 'Touch me properly, sweetheart.'

And though she gasps with desire as she presses right onto my pussy, causing me to gently thrust against her pressure, she slides her hand away to place it back on my thigh. In my ear, she whispers, 'I can't … not here.'

So I whisper, 'OK,' and raise her hand and kiss it, before running the edge of my stiletto up and down her shin and watching her squirm with pleasure. After that, I have to make do with the vibrations of the engine, strumming into my pussy, making me wet.

That's how it is until the taxi drops us off and we scoot into my house as fast as we can. Janey slams the door behind us and collapses against it, then we glance at one another and burst out laughing. 'Oh, God,' gasps Janey, wiping the tears from her eyes, 'this is just too much! No one has a "first date" story like this!'

Lust makes my laughter sink into a sexy smile. In my five-inch peep-toe stiletto heels, I sway towards her like a catwalk model, rolling my hips seductively, keeping her stare on mine. Janey's still smiling as she drinks me in. She pulls off her cap and fans herself with it, before ruffling her hair and tipping her head. The centres of her eyes have gone big and black. I can feel her gaze like melted wax trailing down my front. I'm happy and horny and hopelessly high. 'I don't give a fuck about the job,' I say, when I'm so close that I can feel her breath.

'I know you don't,' says Janey, grabbing me round the waist. 'It's the hottest shot of laissez-faire I think I've ever seen.'

I grab her tie, give it a tug, and run the fingers of my free hand through her hair. She sinks backwards, her head thumping against the door, her hands sinking warmly into my back. 'Kiss me,' she says. 'Make me drunk with it.'

So I do.

And suddenly all the tension of the last couple of weeks comes flooding to the surface – the scent that hangs around her after she's showered, the sweet breathy noises she made with Lil, my hands stroking the curves of her buttocks, the sight of her thrusting a sex toy into her pussy as she luxuriated on her bed … this tension all comes catapulting out of me, slamming into Janey as I press her against the door, then grab her through her shirt and feel her nipples rising under my palms. Oh, I knead her and rip her open, and bathe in the sight of her body – the pallor of it, the sleekness, the tightness of her skin – and I kiss down her neck where she smells of her favourite soap, right down her beautiful bicep and the tip of her butterfly tattoo, play-biting the side of her exquisite breast.

'Oh, fuck,' she gasps, pushing her fingers between my thighs, dipping into my briefs. 'Oh, God, you're so wet,' she whispers. 'Oh, Debs, you're perfect.'

I raise my head, looking right into her face. 'And we haven't even got to the good bit yet.'

She smiles. 'And what might that be?'

I give a wink before taking her by the hand and leading her into the living-room. Once there, I tell her to strip right down to her briefs and sit in my white leather armchair. She looks magnificent, lazing back into the leather, one arm draped across the back. She's sleek but muscular, with high little breasts that I want to grasp hold of and rub and bite and press. She also has tattoos – not just the black butterflies that float around her shoulder, but also a string of words that slope across the very top of her left-hand breast. As I get closer, I stare until the words become clear: We See Things as We Are.

'What does that mean?' I ask, pointing.

'It's from a quote from Anais Nin. "We don't see things as they are, we see them as *we* are."' She adds, 'It's a reminder. For me. Not to assume that I'm always right.'

'I love it,' I say, as I tower in front of her. She smiles and sits upright, tracing a finger round the outline of my briefs. Her touch, so close to my pussy, makes me burn. 'Ready?'

'God, yes,' she says.

So I raise my foot and press the sole of my shoe right into her front, slamming her back into the chair. 'Fuck!' she gasps, astonished, but her gaze soon grows weighty with lust again. And even though I've never been a domme like this before, I feel the power of it flooding my body, pulsing through my sex. Then, when I press the sole of my shoe against her lower belly, digging my stiletto heel between her thighs, she snarls to see it, then groans to feel it; and finally she grabs it and presses it into her sex so that all I can think of is ripping off her briefs and thrusting my stiletto heel deep inside her pussy.

'Will you let me worship you?' she asks.

Worship me? Worship *me*?

Holy smokestack, Kitten, this beautiful girl wants me to play the domme!

So I order her to kneel at my feet in the middle of the living-room floor, kiss my calves and run her fingers over my peep-toe stilettos. I get the most extraordinary rush watching this young woman with her muscular physique touching my shoes as if they are a shrine.

When I give her permission to use her tongue, that's when things get really hot. She starts around my stocking-tops, kissing round the lacy edge where strap and stocking meet; then she works down slowly, teasing my flesh with the heat of her lips, kissing down every inch, running her hands down my calves and giving sweet little moans as she gets closer to my feet. And I can feel every touch, every kiss, every caress – I can feel them in my pussy as if that's where she's touching me. And my pussy feels it too because it grows hotter and hotter, slippery beneath my knickers, desperate to fuck and be fucked.

Finally, she lounges on her front as her buttocks swell from her clingy satin knickers, and she licks her way around the open toe of my peep toe, before licking the leather and kissing the bridge of my foot. 'You're sensational,' she breathes, gaze fixed on my feet. She runs a hand up my stockinged leg and her touch makes me gasp. 'Everything about you is magnificent.'

Kitten, I have never been called magnificent before!

Then she looks up at me, with eyes filled with lust. And it's a fuck-me look, a do-me look, an I'm-your-slave-for-ever look, and suddenly I'm telling her to roll onto her back, so I can take in her gorgeous body. Oh, Kitten! Down on my knees, I caress her throat, her collarbone, the swell of her perfect breasts, the tightness of the flesh there, the hardness of her nipples. And God knows where I get the courage, Kitten, but I straddle her like an Amazon, squeezing her hips between my knees as I rub the slippery gusset of my knickers against her own. I kiss and bite those nipples, as she writhes and gasps, tangling her fingers through my hair. And I'm so turned on to see my saliva on her breasts, shining on her pale skin, gleaming on the rosy tips of her nipples, that I start to buck against her body, my hips going crazy as my pussy fills with pleasure. Oh, I could rut her all night! Oh, I could come all over her! And when she raises her hips, returning my own pressure, and our pussies grind together, I know I could climax then and there.

But I've adored her for so long that I want this to last.

So I say, 'Am I domming you, Janey?'

And she says, 'Of course you are, Mistress.'

'Is that OK?' I ask.

She laughs. 'It's more than OK. But if anything isn't OK, I'll use a safe word.'

That's how we agree 'red' for stop and 'green' for keep going.

But once we've had that conversation, I don't really know where to start. I watch her. She watches me. Then I say, 'Um ...'

She smiles. 'I've been a very bad girl. How about some spanking?'

'Oh,' I say. Then I think about her delicious bottom. 'Yes,' I say, 'spanking. You have been a naughty girl, haven't you?'

So I make her wait on all fours while I kneel on the

carpet. 'Crawl over my lap,' I tell her, and she does so with such slowness, her glare fixed on mine, that I feel like she's the predator and I'm the prey. And maybe that's what makes it so deliciously hot when I suddenly pull her down into my lap, and she gasps like she wasn't expecting it.

And oh, God, Kitten, there's her beautiful bum, rising towards my touch, each cheek so pale and tight and round that I peel down her knickers with a rough desperation and spank her over and over again. My pussy burns more fiercely with every slap, especially when Janey whimpers, turning her head, gazing up with a look of wild delight. I must spank her at least a dozen times ... and sometimes she begs for me to go harder; and sometimes she begs for me to fuck her; and sometimes I'm in such a frenzy that I feel as if I'm slapping *my pussy* – not *her bum* – the burn of a climax building in my *own* knickers. In fact, I honestly feel, with Janey's bare skin against me, and the agony of pleasure in her heavy-lidded eyes, that I could come like an avalanche right now.

But with Janey I want to *earn* it.

Next, I sit in the leather chair with Janey astride my lap, and she is a schoolgirl and I am her stern teacher, and she teases me with her eyes and sucks her fingers tauntingly, saying, 'I'm such bad news, Miss. What are you going to do with me, hmm?' And she pulls her fingers from her mouth, till they are wet with saliva, which she then rubs over her hard pink nipples, so dirtily, so taunt-ingly, that I have to bite my lip to keep from moaning.

But what to do next, Kitten? Me being the domme and all? I need to say something rude, right? I need to do something humiliating, yes? So I tell her that I'm going to clean her out because she's dirty, and I start with her mouth, pushing my own fingers in there, before moving to her sex. There's something so hot about her wet satin knickers that reaching in and finding that slippery hole is simply the cherry on the cupcake, Kitten. Then, when I ease my fingers into her pussy, where she's clenching me and writhing against my touch, she catches my wrist and I feel her shudder around it, her eyelids heavy, her breaths coming fast.

You know, she smells like cream in a saucepan, Kitten, warming up, all sweet and thick – and she shivers like she can't contain herself, Kitten. She purrs and murmurs, 'Dirty girl ...' And feeling her so slick, Kitten, watching her writhing body, and feeling her muscles clench me, Kitten, as if they want to trap me there ... this does something to me – something more than arousal – it makes me a dominatrix, Kitten. It brings me to life.

Suddenly, I make her scrabble from my lap, while I rise, feeling taller than ever. 'Kneel on the carpet,' I tell her. 'Put your fingers in your lap.' Then I reach behind my back and unclip my bra. Janey gives a little gasp as I peel away the satin cups. I stand with a foot resting on her knee – a foot she isn't allowed to touch – while I make a slow show of revealing my breasts. Janey's fingers hover mid-air, as if she doesn't know what to reach for – my nipples, my shoes, my stiletto heel or my scant little briefs, which aren't far from her face.

'I told you,' I say, coolly, 'keep your hands in your lap.' And I fling my bra into her face. She gasps, pulling it from her eyes before fixating on my feet. 'Oh, Christ,' she says, softly. She bites her lip. 'Please let me touch your shoes,' she murmurs. 'Please. And lick your toes. Please let me touch your stockings too. I'll do anything. Anything!'

So I press the sole of my shoe between her breasts, and when she gives a little whimper of longing, I say, 'All in good time.'

I tell her to lie down, and when she is there I stand astride her, my shoes close to her hands. 'Still no touching,' I tell her, as she watches my shoes. And even when I raise my left foot and push my stiletto heel right between her lips, making her suckle it as if she's a child, I still won't let her touch me. Oh, Kitten! Seeing her sucking and licking, as if my heel is some delicious candy, makes my pussy burn so deeply that I touch myself through my briefs. I fuck her mouth faster and faster, watching the excitement growing on her face, and I moan as I feel my clit growing harder. Her lips grow wetter, her eyes widen with amazement, but when I notice that she's touching her pussy, I moan out loud, breaking my cool-headed role.

'You'd touch yourself in front of me?' I ask.

'What are you going to do about it?' she taunts.

So what I do is stand astride her hips with the sole of my stiletto shoe pressing onto her sex, and I press and circle, press and circle, against her clit. She groans and gasps and rolls her head, thumping her fists on the carpeted floor, crying out for me to keep going, pleading with me to never stop, telling me it's good, so good, so very good. And even though I keep having to pause, rest my leg and start again, she doesn't mind the pausing – just keeps begging for more. I get so, so damp with her writhing below me while seeing my shoe rubbing her – and she's wet too, so much so that my sole feels like it's moving on oil as I massage her. This is hot! Oh, so *hot*. I dip my fingers into my underwear as Janey thrusts against me, crying out, her hips bucking wildly, thumping on the floor – and every time I think she's done with coming, she starts bucking again, madly, eyelids flickering as she howls.

All this is delectable. All this is exquisite. All this is hotter than anything I've known.

But the most surprising thing – the thing that takes the biscuit – is when Janey rises to her knees and tells me to lie down, her eyes fierce and catlike. When I'm prone, she kneels next to me and tells me to peel off my knickers. It's my turn to take it, she tells me. She slides off one of my shoes before running her fingers inside it and biting her lip as she gives a sigh of pleasure. Then she turns it so my stiletto heel is pointing at my groin.

I'm so agonised by the sight of her that I try to touch myself – just for some release from this need – but she pushes my hand away and slides her own fingers inside me. I open my mouth and groan to feel her inside but, as I do so, she gives me a wicked smile, raises the shoe towards my face and presses the stiletto heel between my lips. Then she tells me to hold it there. 'Suckle,' she says, and, believe me, I do. I suck on the heel as she fucks me with her fingers and watches me with a burning stare – everything feeling so deliciously dirty that soon my hips are out of control, bucking madly as the climax burns through me, rising, then lulling for a moment, before sweeping me up again. I come and come and keep on coming, as I grit my teeth on the stiletto heel, while her gorgeous thrusting fingers get busy down below. And I'm high as a kite and wet as a river, while the pleasure keeps on surging.

Janey and I lie on the sofa in each other's arms. She smiles and traces my lips, my jawline, my eyebrows. She lays soft kisses on my mouth and hair. It's amazing how soft she is – I'd forgotten softness like this. I suppose I was soft like this when I was younger, but her skin seems particularly unsullied. Flawless, except for those black tattoos that are such a joy to kiss and lick.

178

'What will you do now?' she asks me. 'Are you going to get your job back?'

'Certainly not,' I say. Although I'm lost for other ideas.

Janey says, 'You'd never treat your staff like that if you owned a shoe business.' Then she watches me, a sideways smile on her face, her eyebrows on the rise.

'What are you saying?' I ask, propping myself up. I run my fingers through her supersoft hair.

'Well, what if you opened your own store? What if you invested?'

'I don't have that kind of money, love.'

Janey raises her head and presses her lips on mine. 'I, on the other hand, have thousands tucked away.'

'But that's your inheritance,' I say. 'You can't use that!'

Janey lowers her eyes. She seems piqued for a moment, until she looks at me again. 'What if I wasn't just investing the money for you? What if it was for me? For a dream I have?' She tells me that before her father died, he told her that he was leaving her a whole chunk of money and that she was to use it on her dream – whatever that happened to be.

'You dream of opening a shoe store?' I ask, amazed.

'Does that shock you?' she says. Her cheeks have flushed.

'No!' Then I think about it. 'I mean, yes.' I tell her that I've never met anyone more intelligent than her. She's destined for great things. Not shop work.

'I think owning a shoe store *would* be a great thing,' says Janey, with a smile. 'Besides, I think I deserve to have some fun with my passion.'

So I tell her I'll think about it. And I do. I think about it all night as she lies with me in my bed, as I spoon her from behind, kissing the nape of her neck. I dream about our own shop filled with stilettos of peacock-blue, metallic sheens and black-and-white checks.

And I think about how Janey feels so alive in my arms, and how I recently stripped off in the middle of Pussyfoot, before walking butt-naked through the centre of town. And suddenly the world seems very much my oyster. When, finally, I fall asleep, Kitten, I dream that I am a giantess, with huge, red stilettos that are bigger than houses. I dream of gazing down at the people below, all so sad and troubled in their boring, soulless jobs, that they come for miles just to gaze up at me and press their palms on my high-heeled shoes. Some of them polish little circles with their hankies before watching themselves in the reflection. Young folks climb up my needle-heels and slide down the bridge of my foot, squealing and waving their arms as they fly towards my toes.

But sitting on my shoulder is Janey. And she whispers in my ear, 'Stilettos are whatever you want them to be.'

And she's right.

Printed in Great Britain
by Amazon

29453972R00106